"Marry me."

For one second, Kendry [...] [...] next, she was hurt. Jamie didn't know what he was playing with. He couldn't know how hard she was working toward that nursing degree. Still, to joke about marrying someone was odd. "You had me going there for a minute. I thought you were serious."

"I've never been more serious. Marry me."

"Marriage? We're barely friends."

"We're definitely friends."

"But—" She groped for the right thing to say. What she was hearing was so far from what she could possibly have expected. "You don't marry someone because you're friends."

"You are more than just a friend to me, Kendry."

Dear Reader,

I'm so glad you've picked up my first novel for Harlequin Special Edition. This story is near and dear to my heart, inspired as it was by real heroes. I'm a graduate of West Point, and although my time in the military is over, many of my classmates still serve. Always, they are touched by the children they meet during deployments. One classmate began an organization to help medically challenged children in the war zone where he once served, and his personal mission inspired this book.

You see, I started to wonder "what if?" What if a soldier could bring one of those medically needy orphans home with him? What if that orphaned baby needed an adoptive mother? What if that young mother also turned out to be the right woman to heal that soldier's broken heart?

I hope you are inspired by Jamie's heroism and his bride, Kendry's, determination. If you enjoy the fictional world of West Central Texas Hospital, which is set in the real city of Austin, then please look for the story of Jamie's brother, Braden, in *The Doctor's Former Fiancée,* available February 2014.

Until then, I would love to hear what you think of the first book in The Doctors MacDowell series. You can contact me easily through my website at www.carocarson.com.

Cheers,

Caro Carson

Doctor, Soldier, Daddy

Caro Carson

H HARLEQUIN® SPECIAL EDITION®

Recycling programs
for this product may
not exist in your area.

ISBN-13: 978-0-373-65768-1

DOCTOR, SOLDIER, DADDY

Printed in U.S.A.

Books by Caro Carson

Harlequin Special Edition

Doctor, Soldier, Daddy #2286

*The Doctors MacDowell

CARO CARSON

Despite a no-nonsense background as a West Point graduate and U.S. Army officer, Caro Carson has always treasured the happily-ever-after of a good romance novel. After reading romances no matter where in the world the army sent her, Caro began a career in the pharmaceutical industry. Little did she know the years she spent discussing science with physicians would provide excellent story material for her new career as a romance author. Now, Caro is delighted to be living her own happily-ever-after with her husband and two children in the great state of Florida, a location which has saved the coaster-loving, theme-park fanatic a fortune on plane tickets.

Dedication

With love for Richard,
who knew I would write this book long before I did.

Acknowledgments

I am indebted to my critique partners for keeping me
on track despite distractions and obstacles.
Thank you to my partners and friends, T. Elliott Brown,
Catherine Kean and Nancy Robards Thompson.

Chapter One

"You're letting a baby choose your wife?"

Jamie MacDowell chose not to answer that question. Instead, he contemplated the campfire as he let his brother's outraged tone roll off his back. Braden, his oldest brother, cared. That was the real emotion behind the outrage. Jamie had gotten much better at recognizing emotions in the past two years.

"Hire a nanny for the baby. You don't have to marry anyone." His other brother, Quinn, sounded less outraged—but more condescending.

The sounds of the Texas twilight settling over their parents' land filled the silence as Jamie stretched his legs out. He flicked a glance around the fire. It figured: he'd taken the identical pose as his brothers. Braden, Quinn and now Jamie sat with jean-clad legs stretched out fully, each man with his right cowboy boot crossed over his left. It was funny, really, the subconscious mannerisms families shared.

Two years ago, Jamie would have probably uncrossed his ankles, just to be different. But that was before Afghanistan. Before more than a year spent sewing up soldiers in an army hospital.

Before he'd brought his son, Sam, to the United States.

"A nanny can do the job perfectly well," Quinn continued. "You don't need a wife to take care of a baby."

"To take care of my son," Jamie corrected him. It was going to take his brothers some time to get used to the news that he was a father. He hadn't communicated much while he was deployed. Returning to Texas with a nine-month-old had shocked them all. "Not 'a baby.' My son."

"Right. He can be well cared for by a good nanny."

Jamie uncrossed his ankles. Neither of his brothers were parents. They didn't understand the impact, the complete sea change, of having a child. When he held Sam, Jamie knew that he was holding the most important thing in the world. It was a powerful emotion, one that ultimately made his life utterly simple. What his son needed, Jamie would provide.

His son needed a mother.

Not a nanny.

"I'm working in the E.R.," Jamie said. "You know the hours. What nanny is going to be available nights, days, whole twenty-four-hour periods without notice?"

"Get a live-in nanny." Naturally, Quinn had an immediate answer. He was a cardiologist. That particular species of doctor tended to be very math-oriented. Their world was physics. Pressure, diameter, beats per minute. Black and white.

In contrast, as an emergency physician, Jamie often had to wing it. Thinking on the fly, he came up with theories, tested and discarded them, until he'd diagnosed and stabilized whatever emergency had brought the patient to the hospital.

In Afghanistan, there'd been only one kind of emergency: injury. Some injuries were catastrophic, caused by explosives that destroyed so much of the body, Jamie raced the clock to stop the bleeding and keep the heart beating. Some were minor, a finger sliced open when a rifle was cleaned carelessly. All of them—*all of them*—required stitches. Sewing. Surgery. Jamie had performed more surgery as an emergency physician in the United States Army than many surgeons did in civilian life.

"What if I get deployed again?" Jamie asked both brothers. "Will the nanny guarantee her services for the length of my deployment? Will she write to me about Sam? Send me photos?"

Braden abruptly sat up from his lounging position. "I thought you were back to reserve duty, the one-weekend-a-month thing until your commitment was up. Did you sign a new contract?"

Jamie wanted to smile at the predictability of Braden's response. Like Quinn and himself, Braden was also an M.D., but he ran the research side of a massive corporation. He thought in terms of contracts and legalities, of facts on paper. Like Quinn, Braden saw everything as black and white.

The way their father had seen the world.

Jamie stopped lounging, too. With a firm thunk, he set his half-finished bottle of beer on the dry Texas ground by his chair. He wasn't like his father. Sam would have a better man to raise him.

"I'm in the reserves for another six months. I could be recalled to active duty tonight."

Now Quinn sat up abruptly. Jamie felt their tension as both men looked at him intently.

"It's okay," Jamie said quietly. "It's highly unlikely the army will send me back in the next six months."

Braden dropped his gaze to the crackling fire. "It's not that we aren't proud of you."

"I know. I'm proud to have served, too. There are times I've considered volunteering to go back. There's so much work left to be done there." Work that he'd seen one brave woman undertake. Work to promote literacy in the population. Work to provide health care to the poorest of the poor. Work to end the slavelike conditions in which so many Afghani girls were raised.

Work that had ultimately killed that one brave woman, leaving Jamie to raise Sam alone.

"A nanny's not good enough. I want a wife. If something should happen to me, Sam will still have a legal guardian. An American legal guardian."

"He's your son, Jamie. Do you think we'd let the state put him in an orphanage?"

"No." Jamie was touched. Braden had said *your son*. He, at least, was getting used to the idea of Sam being a Mac-Dowell, not just a baby brought home from a war-torn country. "But Mom's getting a little old to start over again with an infant, and look at you. Both of you. A couple of bachelor doctors with insane working hours. Sam needs a full-time parent."

"Then hire a lawyer and make the nanny his legal guardian." Quinn was still seeing in black and white, apparently, but Jamie had already come up with that theory and ruled it out.

"It's easier to get married. A wife's custody is rarely questioned."

There had been no way to legally marry Sam's mother, not on the American base, nor in any Afghani court or mosque. In the end, after her death, that had meant no locals would claim Sam as their own, either. Jamie had been able to get Sam out of the country by mixing State Department regulations and medical necessity, but if the paperwork ever got scrutinized…

If. He wouldn't worry about that now. And if *If* happened, Sam belonging to an American husband and wife would be beneficial, compared to Sam being the child of a bachelor soldier.

Yes, Sam needed a mother. An American mother. Simple.

"I'm fine with a marriage based on practicality," he told his brothers. "I never planned on getting married for any other reason."

"You're sure about that?" Quinn asked.

Jamie sat back in his camp chair and picked up his beer. He brushed the sandy dirt off the bottom of the bottle. When he'd been in Afghanistan, he'd told himself the dry soil wasn't so different from Texas. He'd even been able to squint at the landscape and imagine himself home, if home had a lot of barbed wire and sandbag bomb shelters.

"I'm sure," Jamie said. "Doctors make lousy husbands— look at Dad. He had no time for Mom. No time for any of us. Without Mom, we wouldn't have had a parent at all. My kid needs a mother."

Braden studied the label on his own beer bottle for a moment. "You're not being fair to Dad. We had those fishing trips."

"Yeah, once a year we'd saddle up the horses and pack up the tents and come out here to spend, what? Four days? With a guy we barely knew."

"Still, he tried."

"Yeah, he would have made a fine uncle. Not my idea of a father. My son is going to have a real parent, someone there for him every day, not just for a camping trip now and then. If something happens to me, he's going to have another parent to finish raising him. I'll be damned if I'll leave him alone in this world. I'm getting married, and that's it."

"Slow down, Jamie. What happens if you find this perfect mother, but then you fall in love with another woman, someone you want for something besides mothering? Are you going to divorce the mother of your child to marry the woman you're crazy about? An affair won't cut it. I don't care what this 'perfect mother' agrees to, she's not going to be a Mrs. MacDowell and willingly turn a blind eye to her husband having an affair."

"I'm not going to cheat on my wife, even if we aren't in that kind of a marriage."

"You need to think this through. I've been in love, Jamie." Braden rarely talked about it, but he'd been engaged once. "It can hit you like a lightning strike."

Jamie stood up and pulled the keys to his truck out of his pocket. "It already did, Braden, it already did."

"But, then—"

"She died. Her name was Amina. She was brilliant. Beautiful. An Afghani woman who translated for me on medical missions. She died during the birth and she left me a son."

Jamie dumped the rest of his beer onto a struggling scrub plant, then chucked the bottle into the bed of his pickup truck. "Lightning won't strike twice."

The shocked silence wasn't what Jamie had intended to cause. He clapped Quinn on the shoulder and used the side of his boot to push his still-full beer cooler toward his brother's camp chair. "You finish these for me this weekend. Mom's been watching Sam long enough. I'm gonna run."

Jamie had been away from his son for nearly two hours, and that was too long.

Braden followed him to the pickup. "Jamie. You never told us about the mother of the baby. Sam is really your child, then? Your biological child?"

Damn it. Even his own brothers hadn't believed Sam was his son. How would he convince the State Department? He needed to be married and have Sam legally adopted by his wife, in case they started asking.

"I'm not in the mood for a big-brother lecture, Braden." He loved his oldest brother. Braden had filled more of a father role for him than their father had, but when it came to his own life, Jamie knew what he was doing. He'd come to the ranch today to let his brothers know what his plans were as a courtesy, not so they could tell him he was wrong to want to secure a second parent for Sam as quickly as possible.

"I'm not lecturing," Braden said in a voice made for lecturing. "When do we meet this not-really-a-wife of yours?"

"I don't know who she is yet." Jamie opened the truck door and stepped up on the running board. "No woman I already know fits the bill."

"No woman will. I can't imagine who is going to want your son and not want you."

Ah, the blind loyalty of family. Braden was certain women would fall all over his little brother. He didn't know that most women gave up pursuing Jamie nowadays. His mourning for Amina showed somehow, he was sure.

His son was the only thing that brought a smile to his face now. As he thought of Sam, Jamie felt himself start to grin. "This isn't about me finding a wife. This is about Sam finding a mother. That's why I'm letting him choose her."

Jamie closed the truck door. As he drove away from the old homestead, a new feeling settled over him. A certainty that he was on the right course. Contentment, almost. He'd loved Amina, and now he loved their son. Building his life around his son's needs was the right thing to do.

He wondered whom Sam would fall in love with. He wondered whom his son would choose for him to marry.

Chapter Two

Kendry Harrison was a general dogsbody. It wasn't the loveliest term, but it accurately summed up her career at West Central Hospital. She'd like to think that she was at least a gopher, but that would imply she worked for someone important who needed her to run errands. No such luck. She was just a general dogsbody, plugged into whatever entry-level job needed doing. Today, she was working in the pediatric ward.

Kendry loved the pediatric ward, even if it broke her heart half the time. Kids were kids, though, and even when they sported IV tubing and wore hospital gowns, they tended to be adorable. Kendry loved their earnestness when they described their little lives. She loved their willingness to play as hard as they possibly could, even when they found themselves forced to use their wrong hand or unable to climb out of a wheelchair.

Unlike the adult patients, the kids were still eager to grab life with both hands—unless they were in pain. Although an infant named Myrna was due to be discharged today, Kendry wondered if the little girl was in pain. Hour after hour, Myrna had been growing quieter and quieter. Kendry's shift was over in only minutes, but she couldn't leave Myrna without trying, one more time, to get the nurse to pay attention to the change in the baby's behavior.

She pushed the button to call the nurses' station. Again.

"What is it this time, Kendry?" The voice over the speaker was clearly irritated.

"I'd like a nurse to check on Myrna Quinones for me, please." If she kept her voice cool and factual, the way the doctors and nurses spoke, then she would be taken more seriously. Unfortunately, her nose was stuffy, and she barely grabbed a tissue in time for a sneeze.

"We've checked on her every hour. She's fine. She'll be going home when her mother gets off work today." And then, with the most sarcastic version of sugary sweetness the nurse could muster, her tinny voice came over the speaker. "And you're officially off work now, so go on home, darlin'. Take something for that cold, or you'll get all the children sick."

"I'm fine, thank you," Kendry said through clenched teeth. "It's just allergies."

She was the only adult in the pediatric ward's playroom, making it impossible for her to leave, but she resisted the urge to point that out to the nurse. Instead, she released the intercom's talk button and went to the sink to wash her hands for the fiftieth time of the day.

Every young patient who was able spent a good part of his or her waking hours in the ward's colorful playroom. There were hard plastic chairs and tables that could be sprayed down with bleach, plenty of floor space for children to play while they tugged along their wheeled poles with their hanging IV bags. A few of the children were not patients, but were the children of staff members. As long as the child wasn't contagious, staff members could pay a small fee to have their child spend the day in the playroom when their regular childcare fell through—a benefit that made West Central Texas Hospital one of Austin's top-rated employers.

For doctors, the policy was even more lenient. If it meant doctors would show up for every shift, the hospital was happy to provide childcare. These kids Kendry got to know well. One of them, a little charmer named Sammy, was demanding her attention now, as he often did.

Kendry scooped him off the floor and settled him on her hip. "That's right, Sammy. It doesn't matter if I'm off the clock, I'm not going home and leaving Myrna here in this condition, now am I?"

Sammy didn't get a chance to coo or babble an answer to her, because the person scheduled to replace Kendry had arrived and was listening in.

"Which one's Myrna?" she asked.

Kendry thought her replacement was kidding. For a second. One look at the woman's face—Paula, she remembered—revealed that she wasn't.

"Myrna is the little girl whose hand I'm holding. She was technically discharged because we were short beds, but her mother has to work, so admin said she could stay here." The little girl's belongings were packed in a plastic bag and her IV lines had been removed upon discharge, but her crib had been wheeled into the playroom until her mother could come to pick her up. Her room had already been filled by another patient.

"What time is her mother supposed to arrive?"

"Not for another hour. I don't want to leave Myrna like this."

Paula frowned at the baby in the stainless-steel hospital crib. "Like what? Calm and peaceful? Lord help me, I hope they all get like that and stay like that."

Kendry couldn't force herself to chuckle along with Paula's joke, although she knew that was what was expected of her. "Myrna's been here all week. Don't you realize this isn't her normal disposition?"

Paula shot Kendry a look. "Well, excuse me, Miss Know-It-All. There's a lot of kids in here, and they change every day."

Dang it. Now Kendry had taken the attention off the little girl and unwittingly put it on herself. Paula, unlike Kendry, was a certified medical assistant, a CMA. There was always a CMA on duty overnight. Paula was higher up on the hospital ladder, and Kendry had offended her.

"You're so right. The ward has been at full occupancy all week." Kendry could swallow her pride with the best of them when it came to helping a child. Heck, when it came to nearly every aspect of her life. "Myrna Quinones is acting like she's fighting an infection, maybe. Something is making her listless."

Paula pressed the call button for the nurses' station, announcing herself as she did so. "Hey, it's Paula here. Have you gotten a temperature on this Quinones child?"

The tinny response sounded exasperated. "Of course we have. Her vitals have been normal every single time we've checked them. Tell that orderly to go home. There's no budget for overtime around here. She should have clocked out five minutes ago."

Paula wasn't here five minutes ago, so I couldn't have clocked out.

Kendry spoke to Sammy, who sat on her hip as he chewed his fingers. "Let's go for a walk, little guy. We'll clock me out, then come back to say bye-bye to Myrna."

The lively little boy on her hip cheerfully called, "Da-da!"

Sammy's dad was here. Kendry knew what *Da-da*'s voice would sound like. She braced herself for that educated, masculine timbre, that voice with just a hint of native Texas drawl.

"Hey, little buddy. How was your day?"

It didn't matter how many times she heard it, it still made her melt a little. Sammy kicked Kendry vigorously in happy response as she turned around to find Sammy's father, all six-feet-something of him, standing close enough to take his son out of her arms.

"Hi, Dr. MacDowell. Sammy's doing well today. He drank every ounce of formula. He seems to have an easier time taking his bottle when I have him sitting almost straight up. It makes me wonder if—"

"Good evening, Dr. MacDowell." Paula's voice had a different tone to it now. All peaches and cream.

Kendry stifled her frustration. She wanted to discuss Sam's ability to eat, but Paula wanted to…to…

Flirt. There wasn't a woman in the hospital who didn't know Dr. MacDowell was single. Never had been married, apparently. He'd returned from military service in Afghanistan with Sammy, so the rumor mill said, and had turned in his camouflage for a civilian career in order to spend more time with his son. Because no mother was in the picture, some people speculated that the baby was an orphan whom Dr. MacDowell had adopted. This only made women sigh with even more approval.

Sammy grabbed the tubing of Dr. MacDowell's stethoscope and tried to get it—and his fist—in his mouth. The doctor calmly pried the baby's fingers open, removed the stethoscope from around his neck and tucked it into the pocket of his white lab coat, all in one smooth move. Then he dropped a kiss on top of Sammy's head.

He was Sammy's father, all right. Who cared if the baby's hair was a darker black than his father's deep brown? Who cared if the child seemed petite compared to his strapping American father? This baby was loved. Kendry wished all the children that came through West Central were so lucky.

"You can go home now, Kendry," Paula said.

"What were you saying about Sam's bottles?" Dr. Mac-Dowell asked.

"I'm wondering if—"

"I've got his daily sheet right here, with all his feedings listed," Paula interrupted. "Kendry, you need to go clock out. There's no overtime in the budget, and you don't want to tick off the supervisor."

Kendry wished her Irish heritage didn't make it so easy for her pale skin to blush. She hated being put in her place, but even more, she hated being so firmly reminded she was an hourly-wage orderly in front of Dr. MacDowell.

"I'll walk with you, Miss Harrison," Dr. MacDowell said. "I want to hear what you have to say."

Miss Harrison. He addressed everyone in the hospital by their proper names and titles. Still, she couldn't help but appreciate the respect he showed her. He wanted to hear what she had to say. He always did. He was the kind of doctor who would patiently listen to family members who anxiously brought someone to the E.R. He would listen…

Her gaze returned to Myrna, who was lying as she'd been for the past hour. She hadn't responded to Paula or Dr. Mac-Dowell's appearance by her crib.

Dr. MacDowell would listen.

"Could you look at this patient for me? Her name is Myrna Quinones, she's nine months old, and she's due to be discharged today. She had surgery three days ago, and I'm wondering if she might have an infection or something. She's grown increasingly listless today, and I haven't been able to interest her in taking more than a couple of ounces from her bottle, but she's been off IV fluids since this morning. Maybe she's dehydrated?"

"Kendry, please." Paula sounded shocked. "You don't bother physicians with cases that aren't theirs. Dr. MacDowell, I assure you, the nurses on the floor have been checking on Myrna every hour. I've requested an update myself, and she isn't running a fever or showing any signs of infection."

"Thank you, Mrs. Cook."

Kendry bit her lower lip. Dr. MacDowell had said *thank you* in that dismissive tone doctors seemed to master, the one that said *when I want your opinion, I'll ask for it*. Kendry saw Paula call for the floor nurse with a press of a button. Once the nurses realized a doctor was checking the patient, they'd show up. Doctors were at the opposite end of the food chain from orderlies.

"Could you hold Sammy for me, please?" Dr. MacDowell asked.

Kendry held out her arms for the little boy, who dove right into them. Dr. MacDowell took his stethoscope out of his pocket and slung it around his neck. As he walked the few steps to the hand sanitizer station, he asked Kendry questions briskly, impersonally. Normal fluid intake? Number of wet diapers today? Normal activity level?

Then he was bending over the crib, opening Myrna's hospital gown, listening to her chest, running strong hands over the baby's limbs, feeling for pulse points. *Thank you,* Kendry wanted to say. *Thank you, thank you, thank you.*

The baby seemed fine, if unnaturally calm. The doctor didn't seem to be finding anything out of the ordinary. Kendry started to feel absurd.

"Is it possible to have an infection without running a fever?" she asked.

"No," Paula answered.

"Yes," Dr. MacDowell said. "Which procedure did this child have?"

Kendry waited a beat for Paula to answer, but Paula obviously didn't know and gestured toward Kendry with one hand.

"It was a kidney repair of some kind. I believe they

opened a blocked tube, but whether it was going into the kidney or leading out, I'm not sure."

Dr. MacDowell opened the baby's diaper and palpated her pelvis and bladder. "Did you recently change her diaper?"

"It's been hours. I keep checking, but it's dry."

"Her bladder's distended. Mrs. Cook, I want this patient transported to the E.R. Get Dr. Gregory on the phone for me."

"Yes, Doctor."

Dr. MacDowell gently flipped the baby over and removed her incision bandages. Some unhealthy pus oozed from the tiny incision site. Kendry had never been so sorry to be proved so right.

Dr. MacDowell did not look happy. At all.

"I'm sorry," Kendry said. "I'm an orderly. I'm not allowed to remove a patient's bandage."

"No, but the nurses are," he said, and she didn't think she was imagining the quiet anger in his voice. "They should have, given your report."

For the first time in her memory, Kendry was suddenly glad she wasn't a nurse. No doubt Paula felt the same as she handed the phone to Dr. MacDowell. "Dr. Gregory on the line for you."

Kendry busied herself by packing up Sam's diaper bag with one hand as she held him on her hip with the other. Then she quieted another fussy baby, feeling soothed herself as she listened to Dr. MacDowell updating Dr. Gregory on the patient he was sending his way. One of her fellow orderlies arrived to wheel Myrna downstairs to the E.R.

Paula hissed in Kendry's ear as the crib was being rolled away. "Get off the clock before you get in trouble for going over."

"Here, hold Sammy then."

But Sammy wouldn't go to Paula. He clung to Kendry's

neck as fiercely as any nine-month-old could, which was pretty darned hard.

Paula tried, anyway, pitching her voice to a falsetto coo. "Come on, Sam, let Miss Paula hold you." She started prying Sammy's small fingers off Kendry's neck, which only served to make the child more desperate to cling to the adult of his choice.

Dr. MacDowell hung up the house phone and came over to intercede. "Hey, buddy, come see Daddy."

Sam was in full-pitch tantrum mode now. He wanted to cling to Kendry's neck, and by God, that's what he was gonna do.

"He usually comes to me," Dr. MacDowell said, frowning.

Kendry patted the baby's back and fought her urge to back away from Paula and Dr. MacDowell. She interjected a deliberate note of cheerfulness into her voice. "That's okay—it's okay. Shh, Sammy." She gave Paula's arm a pat to get her to stop clawing at the child's fingers, then started bouncing Sammy gently. "Just let him catch his breath. He'll be fine. He needs a second to decide what to do next."

Paula dropped her hand.

Dr. MacDowell spread his large hand over his son's back and stayed that way. "Okay, buddy," he said to Sammy. "Okay."

"I think he picked up on the tension. He knew I was worried about Myrna. Thank you again for taking a look at her."

"That was a good catch on your part. You were going to tell me something about Sam's bottles?"

From the corner of her eye, Kendry saw Paula turn away and start the closing routine for the playroom, although it would be a couple of hours before she'd bring the last children back to their regular beds for the night.

"It takes Sam a lot longer to finish a bottle than the other kids."

"It does?" His hand stilled on Sammy's back.

Kendry nodded. "I don't think he's just a slow eater. I think he has a hard time swallowing. I tried feeding him almost sitting up today, and he got that bottle down so much faster. You might want to try it yourself and see if that works for you."

"I will. Thanks." The man was really frowning now. Kendry could tell he was mentally recalling feeding sessions with his son, reviewing them for anomalies.

Such a doctor.

"I had no idea he was slower than the other kids," he said, sounding less like a doctor, more like an apologetic, perhaps a little bit defensive, father.

"I guess if you'd never fed another baby, you wouldn't." Kendry smiled at him, not wanting him to feel badly about himself. Sammy helped her out by choosing that moment to decide to turn his face toward his father. The steady, adult conversation had given Sam the chance to calm down enough to realize that he did, indeed, want Daddy.

"Da-da," he said, and twisted his whole little body away from Kendry to grab his father's lapel.

Dr. MacDowell easily took the child's weight from Kendry. "Hey, son. Let's go home. Can you say 'bye-bye' to Miss Harrison?"

But as Dr. MacDowell shifted a step back from Kendry, Sammy reached his hand out for her. "Me," he said. His little fist opened and closed, stretched out toward her. "Me."

"Bye-bye, Sammy. I'll see you again real soon." Kendry wished she could drop a kiss on his soft hair, but she wasn't supposed to kiss the children. It was against hospital policy, for health-related reasons. Besides, she'd end up with her face way too close to the doctor's face. She imagined the sensation of brushing cheeks with him—

That was best saved for another time.

No, that was best saved for never. It would never be a good time to imagine the feel of Dr. MacDowell's skin.

It would be warm.

Stop it.

Kendry settled for a smile, then bent to pick up her bag. When she straightened, Dr. MacDowell hadn't left, but looked like he was waiting on her. For a second, for one insane second, Kendry thought that the handsome man with that adorable child was waiting to spend more time with her.

"Can I walk you to your car?" he asked.

Kendry wanted to melt on the spot. He was such a gentleman. Too bad she didn't have a car for him to walk her to.

No, she was Kendry Ann Harrison, minimum-wage-earning hourly employee, the girl who rode the city bus because she'd once been too stupid to go to college when she'd had the chance. She didn't belong with the guy who'd devoted a decade of his life to learning all the medical know-how that allowed him to save people's lives.

"Thanks, but I have to go clock out. Have a good night."

She slung her tote bag over her shoulder and headed out of the room with what she hoped was a cheerful, unembarrassed, jaunty attitude.

"Me," Sammy said, drawing out the syllable in a high-pitched voice of distress.

Kendry almost stopped. She knew that when Sammy wanted something, he said "me" instead of "mine." But since she was Kendry, and his father was Dr. MacDowell…well, she wasn't his mother, and he wasn't her baby.

Still, she turned to blow her favorite baby a kiss over her shoulder.

The juggling routine never varied.

Jamie thought he ought to be getting better at it by now, but he still felt like a caricature of a single parent, the kind on TV commercials who dropped briefcases and seemed incapable of balancing babies and bottles. If only there were a solution at the end of thirty seconds of failure, like on TV. If only Jamie could press a door-opening button on the key to a certain car, or spot some golden arches that would magically make his day easier.

The juggling only got worse in real life. This evening, it was raining, but Jamie couldn't pull his car into the garage, which was still full of boxes from his deployment. He dashed with Sam from the driveway to the side door, but the door refused to open. The days of uncharacteristic rain had made the wood swell, so Jamie ended up kicking open the door while Sam cried and the rain pelted them both.

"I know, Sam, I know. We'll get you out of these wet clothes ASAP. They get cold real quick when they're wet, don't they?" Jamie kept his monologue running as he tried to keep the arm that was holding Sam inside the house while reaching out into the rain with his other arm to retrieve both his briefcase and the fallen diaper bag. "I can fix the clothes thing, son. Give me a second to shove this door closed, and I can fix that one problem. Thank God."

Sam didn't seem convinced, judging by the misery on his face and the volume of his cries.

Jamie applied some force to get the door to shut. In the still of the house, he could hear the rain dripping from the bottom of the diaper bag. The denim was soaked. One more thing he'd need to fix before his next shift at the hospital. Unpack the diaper bag, throw it in the dryer, repack it before work.

Damn. He let his head drop back to rest on the wall, let the denim drop onto the wood floor, which was wet, anyway.

His daily life wasn't difficult, really, just a constant to-do list of tasks. So why did he feel so overwhelmed by it all sometimes?

Maybe his brother was right. Maybe having a nanny waiting for him now would be the solution. A grandmotherly woman, ready to put the diaper bag in the dryer for him. A gray-haired lady who would have had the lights on in the house while she waited for him to come home. One of the nanny services he'd consulted had specified light cooking as an option in their contract. There could be supper waiting for him now, made by a sweet old lady.

Even when he was dripping wet and tired, Jamie didn't like the image. He didn't want a grandmotherly person in his house, someone to accommodate, someone to adjust to.

He wanted a partner, a peer, someone who would love Sam like her own, day after day, year after year, with no salary and no vacations. A mother for Sam, not for himself. Was it too much to ask?

Sam wailed.

"Right. It's just you and me, kid. Dry clothes, coming right up."

Chapter Three

Jamie struggled with his guilt while his son struggled with his bottle.

When all the little things went wrong, one after another, when Jamie's workday had been long and his baby refused to be comforted, memories of Amina brought him no comfort. On days like those—on days like today—instead of missing Amina, instead of wishing she were here to share the safe life of suburban America, Jamie would feel angry.

Amina could have shared this life. Amina could have seen their son growing day by day, but she'd chosen a different route, a path in life that had led to her death. She'd left Jamie alone to pick up the pieces, to protect her baby, to keep her memory alive for their son. And sometimes, damn it all to hell, Jamie was pissed off at the choices she'd made.

Being pissed off at a dead woman was unacceptable. The guilt was heavy on him now. It felt familiar.

He and Sam were dry, at least, both wearing white T-shirts and sitting together in the leather recliner. Jamie hadn't been able to find a rocking chair that fit his size comfortably, and the recliner did the trick when it came to relaxing with the baby until Sam—or both of them—fell asleep.

Tonight, though, as Sam worked his way through swallowing and spitting up the contents of his bedtime bottle, relaxation seemed a long way off. Sometimes Jamie thought he'd never relax again—not for the next eighteen years, anyway. Not while he was the sole adult responsible for making sure Sam had all he needed for a good life.

Usually, these quiet moments with his son made everything fall into place. The troubles of his workday receded, unable to keep his attention when he held this baby and felt all the wonderment of a new life.

Usually, but not tonight.

As Sam grunted and sucked his way through the bottle, Jamie studied his son's face. Sam looked like Amina. His arrestingly dark eyes were undoubtedly his mother's. Jamie smoothed a hand over the soft, black hair on Sam's head—also Amina's. He let Sam curl his hand around Jamie's index finger. Those fingers didn't look like Jamie's. Nor his toes. Did they look like Amina's?

Jamie no longer remembered details like that, the shape of her thumb or pinky finger. He was forgetting. If he forgot Amina, there would be nobody to tell Sam about his mother. Amina had been the last of her family, the sole survivor when the rest had been wiped out by the war. For resisting the Taliban, her family name had been erased to the last distant cousin. Amina had only been spared by a matter of days, she'd told him, sent to school in London before the slaughter in her village had taken place.

Jamie wondered how the MacDowells would have reacted if the local sheriff suddenly had the power to walk onto their ranch and start shooting. His family probably would have been as defiant as Amina's family had been. Perhaps that was one reason he and Amina had hit it off so quickly. They were kindred spirits. She could have been a MacDowell.

She *should* have been a MacDowell.

Instead, even while she was pregnant with Jamie's child, she'd chosen to stay in a country where prenatal care was nonexistent. Hell, indoor plumbing was still a sign of personal wealth. Against Jamie's medical advice and personal plea, she'd obstinately traveled with a documentary film crew. In a remote village, she'd gone into premature labor while on her crusade to persuade Afghanis to let their daughters attend school. She'd died not from a Taliban bullet like the rest of her family, but from a lack of medical care, like too many women in her country.

Tonight, Jamie was angry at a woman who'd lost her entire family years before she, herself, had died.

More guilt.

Sam worked greedily at his bottle.

No, Amina's family weren't all dead. Sam was here, and Jamie would do everything to ensure one member of that brave family had a life that didn't end in tragedy.

Jamie bent his head as he lifted Sam's tiny hand and planted a kiss on the perfectly formed fingers. If they weren't his fingers and they weren't Amina's fingers, whose were they? A bit of DNA passed on from a great-grandparent? Or did those fingers, perhaps, come from another man, a man who had come into Amina's life before Jamie?

More guilt for even thinking such a thought.

Jamie had too much time to think about things in the safety of his quiet ranch house. Afghanistan had been intense—life outside the wire more so. Emotions ran high, bonds were formed quickly, and Amina, his unit's translator and general ambassador to the local population, had literally slipped into his bed after they'd worked together for only two short weeks.

At the time, he hadn't been surprised. They'd had chemistry and a connection from their first meeting. For the first two weeks, they'd spent nearly every moment together, seeking out the smallest villages and encampments, offering medical care to the local population. Amina's intelligence and her determination to better her fellow countrymen had made an impact on Jamie, if not on the villagers.

He hadn't been surprised that Amina was sexually experienced, either, because she'd lived in London longer than she'd lived with her family in Afghanistan. Her appearance was Afghani, but her personality was Western. He'd fallen for her and she for him. When, in the dark hours before dawn, she'd silently come into the hut he used as both clinic and bedroom, he'd had no doubts as she'd slipped into his bed.

Now, however, thousands of miles away and a year and a half later, he wondered. Had she already been pregnant? Had she wanted Jamie to believe he was the father, so that her son would have an American protector?

Sam gurgled down a few swallows of formula and patted Jamie's hand with his own. Jamie clutched the baby closer to his chest.

If Amina had wanted an American soldier to protect her coming baby, she'd gotten one. Jamie would never let Sam go, whether they shared DNA or not. The feel of this child in his hands was essential to his life. It had been from the moment a local midwife who'd trekked miles on foot stood outside the barbed wire and handed him a dehydrated newborn and the news that Amina was dead. Dead and already buried, in accordance with their laws.

And so Jamie had sworn on a legal document that Sam was his biological child. He'd gotten the required signatures of others in his military unit, fellow soldiers and civilian contractors who could vouch that they'd seen Jamie working with Amina the eight months before the birth of the child, an appropriate period of time that could make it possible for Jamie to be the father. If any of those witnesses had wondered how an infant born at only eight months of gestation had appeared to be full-term, they'd kept that to themselves as they'd scrambled to help Jamie find formula and bottles—a futile search.

IVs had kept Sam alive those first critical days. Jamie had still had a week left on his tour of duty, but he'd literally wheeled Sam's stretcher onto the next medical flight to Germany. No one had questioned him. Jamie had gambled that forgiveness would be easier to gain than permission, and that gamble had paid off.

So far.

But in the quiet of nights like tonight, as Jamie looked at the son who looked nothing like him, fear crept into his chest. What if the State Department got around to that paperwork and a diligent clerk decided to order medical tests to prove the baby biologically belonged to the soldier?

The blood-type test would be ordered first. If the blood types were incompatible, then the soldier could not be the father of the child. If the blood types were compatible, it only proved that it was possible for the soldier to be the father, but the paternity was still in question.

Jamie knew his blood type. He knew Sam's. It was *possible* that he was Sam's father. But it was not a fact, not without further DNA testing, and if the State Department chose to order those tests…

He willed the fear away. Jamie sat Sam up to pat his back, hoping that air bubbles would come up but formula would stay down. It was a struggle at every feeding. The nurse at the hospital playroom had said that Sammy had more problems with the bottle than other babies in her care. That nurse seemed particularly bright, the one with the ponytail and glasses.

No—the young woman was not a nurse. She was an orderly. Jamie had noticed her before, when she'd worked in the emergency room. The orderly was certainly working in the right field; she had a natural talent for noticing patients' needs. She'd been working in the pediatric playroom more and more often, something Jamie had been glad to see. Sammy was in good hands when that particular woman was on duty.

"Come on, Sammy, give me a burp to make any college frat boy proud."

Instead, Sammy vomited a substantial amount of formula over the blanket that Jamie had laid over his lap. The formula wasn't curdled, not even partially digested. What went down came right back up, every feeding.

Sammy had been born with a birth defect, a hole in the wall of his heart. It would be repaired soon, and Sam would grow up never knowing it had been there. That particular birth defect shouldn't cause feeding issues. Jamie had assumed all this spitting up was normal, but now the orderly— Miss Harrison was her name—had said Sam needed to sit up to drink his bottle.

As he soothed Sam by rubbing his back, Jamie's medical training kicked in automatically. *Consider the options. Eliminate them one by one.*

What conditions caused a baby to need to be fed upright? Cleft palate? Jamie tapped his index finger to Sam's perfect, bow-shaped lips. Obviously, Sammy didn't have a cleft palate.

Jamie tried to feed Sam a few more ounces of formula, this time sitting him far more upright. It did make a difference. He could feel Sam's body relaxing as the ounces went down with less struggle. Was this how most babies fed, then? Settling in, relaxing, not fighting to get each swallow?

This time, when Jamie burped Sam, he slipped his finger in his son's mouth and felt the palate. The roof of the baby's mouth was there, intact. Of course, this had been checked early in Sam's life, part of the routine exam Ameri-

can doctors gave all newborns. Jamie had flashed his pen-
light down his son's throat more than once. The roof of his
son's mouth was fine, intact on visual inspection. This time,
Jamie pressed a little harder, moved a little more slowly,
working his way toward the throat, millimeter by millimeter.

Sam objected, but Jamie concentrated as he would with
any patient. He kept palpating despite Sam's whines and
wiggles—and then he felt the roof of the mouth give. The
palate wasn't formed correctly toward the back of the throat.
It looked normal because the membrane covering the roof
of the mouth had grown over it, but there was a definite
cleft, hidden.

Miss Harrison had noticed a symptom that Sam's pe-
diatricians and Jamie himself had missed. Sam had a cleft
palate. A very slight, easily overlooked, but definitely mal-
formed palate. One that hindered his swallowing.

Guilt.

If any parent should have figured that out, he should have.
He was an M.D., but this was his first child, the first baby
he'd ever given a bottle to, and it hadn't occurred to him
that the amount of formula that came back up was greater
than normal.

Like the doctor he was, his brain kept working despite the
guilt. After the diagnosis, treatment options needed to be
reviewed. As medical problems went, this one was simple.
Sammy would have to go under the knife one more time,
but it was fixable.

"Me," Sammy whined, reaching toward the empty bottle. "Me!"

"This is what you want, little buddy?"

Jeez, his kid was probably hungry, ready to eat more, now
that he could get it down and keep it down, thanks to Miss
Harrison figuring out the best position.

"Me."

"Got it. Coming right up." Jamie carried Sam into the

kitchen, tossing the balled-up dirty blanket into the laundry room as he went, then started the process of opening the can of formula.

Jamie owed Miss Harrison more than a simple thank-you. He could write her a commendation, although the possibility for a raise or a promotion was slim when the hospital was under a strict budget.

"Me." Sammy grabbed for the freshly filled bottle.

Jamie chuckled to himself. "Yes, this is yours. Trust me, I don't want it."

At least his son did well communicating. He was advanced for his age when it came to expressing his needs verbally, as he was doing now. "Me" was an effective way for the baby to say he wanted something. He'd used it earlier today, when Jamie had come to pick him up at the hospital day-care center. Sam had wanted—

Jamie stopped in the middle of the living room.

Sam had wanted Miss Harrison.

Chapter Four

Jamie MacDowell, emergency room physician and war veteran, very nearly chickened out.

Last night's revelation that Sam was attached to Miss Harrison warranted further investigation at his first opportunity, but when Jamie spotted her sitting alone in the hospital cafeteria, he felt like a boy in sixth grade, ready to turn tail and run rather than sit next to a girl.

The cashier charged the lunch to Jamie's account. Instead of looking toward Miss Harrison's table, Jamie made eye contact with the cartoonish scarecrow that was taped to the cash register for the fall. In four weeks, Jamie would be reporting to his reserve unit for two days of military training.

For the next six months, he'd report once a month, train for two days and come back home. Unless, of course, the medical unit was activated and deployed to Afghanistan, or any other corner of the world where they were needed. Jamie would go, and Sam would be left behind.

Sam needed a mother.

With a brief nod at the cashier and a fresh sense of determination, Jamie picked up the plastic cafeteria tray in one hand and turned toward Miss Harrison's corner of the cafeteria. Sam's favorite caregiver sat, alone, at one of the smaller tables. She was concentrating on her meal, so Jamie studied her face as he approached. He'd thought of her as plain, but she wasn't homely. If they shared a house, it wouldn't be a punishment to look at her across a dinner table. She had even features. Her mouth was compressed into a bit of a frown right now, but her lips were pink and not too full, not too thin.

Not that it matters. Mothers were always beautiful to their children, and this woman might make a good mother. He was here to find out.

"Is this seat taken?"

She looked up at him and froze for a moment, her spoon halfway to her mouth, before she glanced toward the entrance to the physician-only dining room.

"I'm not required to eat in the physicians' lounge." He smiled at her and stood there like an idiot, holding his tray. Middle school had never been this uncomfortable. "May I join you?"

She nodded, so he sat.

"Thanks," he said. "I thought you'd like to know how your dialysis patient was doing today."

"You mean Myrna?"

Jamie silently awarded her a point in her favor. She knew each child in her care by name. The patients were more to her than their pathologies.

"Was the incision site infected only near the surface, or had it spread outward from her kidney?" she asked.

"It appears to be localized at the incision site. Her kidneys are clear." Jamie was glad she understood the pathology, however, because his son had his share of medical issues. The kids whose parents were the best informed tended to be the kids who did well. Another point in her favor. "It was caught early, thanks to you."

"I'm glad to hear it, Dr. MacDowell."

"Call me Jamie."

For a split second, she looked at him like he'd just suggested they go somewhere and get naked. Dropping titles could indicate that kind of intimacy in a hospital setting, he knew. The next second, she turned her head and sneezed. Loudly.

Her nose seemed to be perpetually runny, although it was a nice enough nose, besides being red most of the time. She turned away from the table and blew her nose rather unbecomingly. With purpose. Force. Her bangs fell over her face, got tangled with the napkin she was using to mop up.

Jamie pushed aside his mashed potatoes and congealed gravy.

"Excuse me," she said, when she was done with a second napkin.

"No problem." Physical attraction to her would make their co-parenting awkward, anyway.

She was having soup and crackers. Lots of crackers. She had a tower of those little oyster cracker packets on her tray. He tried to see through them to the photo ID that hung on the lanyard around her neck, hoping to catch a glimpse of her first name. It seemed awkward to have to ask a woman her first name when she already knew his child as well as he did. Better than he did, in some ways. Her name tag stayed wrong way out.

"Have you worked here long, Miss Harrison?"

She turned away and sneezed again. At least it flipped her name tag around.

Kendry. Kendry Harrison. Jamie waited for a feeling of great portent to settle over him. Waited for a thunderbolt to strike, for a feeling of destiny, for something.

"Amina. Amina Sadat." She'd laughed, and in a voice

*that blended foreign tones with British enunciation, she'd
said, "At least, that's the Westernized version of my name."
She'd then recited a sentence-long string of syllables, her
true Afghani name, one he would later learn included her
father, her grandfather and nearly her whole family tree.
Every syllable had sounded like exotic music...*

Jamie cleared his throat. "Kendry? That's an unusual
name. What country is it from?"

She dabbed at her nose with her crumpled napkin, an
apologetic motion. "I think my parents made it up. They're
kind of free-spirited like that."

Free-spirited parents? Not the kind of people he expected,
somehow, to produce the plain, serious person in front of
him.

"But to answer your first question, I've been working
here for nearly six months."

Another point for her. She wasn't distracted easily. Which
reminded him that he needed to keep his head in the game.
He was here to gauge their compatibility. "Do you enjoy
working in the hospital?"

"Yes, I do." Her eyebrows drew together, frowning at
him as she met his gaze. Her eyes were sort of a nondescript
greenish hazel. "Why do you ask?"

"I couldn't imagine working in any other environment,
but not everyone feels the same."

"How does it compare to working in a hospital in the
Middle East? Is it true that you were in the military?"

He hadn't intended to talk about himself, but fifteen minutes later, when Kendry stood and said her lunch break was
over, Jamie realized she'd learned more about his life history than he had about hers.

"Can we do lunch again tomorrow?" he asked.

Her water glass rattled on her tray as she jerked to a sudden standstill. "Was there something else you needed to talk
to me about? Something about Sam, maybe?"

He hoped his smile was casual. "Sam is my favorite topic. Let's meet tomorrow and discuss Sam."

She hesitated, looking oddly vulnerable in her plain green scrubs, holding her tray tightly with two hands. "Is there any trouble? Anything I should be aware of?" she asked.

"Trouble?" He hadn't meant to worry her.

"Am I doing something that could…that could mean I might be…" She took a deep breath and stoically asked, "Dr. MacDowell, am I in danger of losing my job?"

The way she asked it—the fact that she would ask such a thing at all—set some kind of alarm off inside him. Why would she jump to a conclusion like that?

Damn, he was going to have to hire a private investigator. It would have been the first thing his brother Quinn would have done, long before any kind of getting-to-know-you lunch. Jamie was a fool to begin by simply spending time with the woman his son preferred.

Kendry was waiting for his answer, her whole posture stiff and solemn.

"You're not in any trouble that I know of," he said. "Are you on probation for any misconduct?"

"I'd never do anything to jeopardize this opportunity. Not intentionally. But Paula told me I overstepped my bounds by asking you to check on Myrna Quinones yesterday."

Jamie leaned back in his plastic chair and studied her. Judging by the way her brows were drawn and her eyes watched him intently, she was either terribly concerned or terribly offended. The emotion brought a spark to her eyes, and he noticed now they were much more than a plain hazel. They were sharp, intelligent, expressive.

"I'm glad you did. You made a difference in Myrna's outcome. Any child would be fortunate to have someone like you watching out for him."

"Oh. Well, thank you." She stood there for another moment, tray in hand, and Jamie wondered if she felt as awkward as he had. "I've got to go. If I don't clock in on time, I really could be in trouble."

"See you tomorrow, then," he said, and he watched her walk away. She blended easily into the crowd of scrub-wearing personnel.

Yet, Sammy had singled her out.

Jamie glanced at the paper pumpkin decorations dangling from the cafeteria ceiling. Four weeks. He had four weeks to get to know Sammy's favorite caregiver. And maybe, just maybe, he had four weeks to persuade her to marry him.

What on earth had that been all about?

Kendry dumped her tray on the cafeteria conveyor belt and made a beeline for the elevators. She had to get to the hospital's basement and clock in within the next three minutes.

Her thoughts raced as she practically speed-walked down the corridor. Dr. MacDowell had eaten lunch with her. Sammy's daddy, the one who made her heart race when they accidentally touched while passing Sammy between them at pickup time. Physicians rarely ate in the main cafeteria, for starters, but for the hospital's most handsome and eligible doctor to single her out, to choose to sit at her table, was truly odd.

Kendry waved the bar code on her ID tag in front of the time clock's scanner with seconds to spare. According to the list tacked to the employee bulletin board, she was needed in the pediatric ward's playroom this afternoon. Dr. Mac-Dowell had eaten lunch with her, so Sammy would be in the playroom. There was a silver lining to today's bizarre lunch.

She rode the elevator to the pediatric floor of the hospital, feeling her spirits rise at the prospect of spending the afternoon with Sammy and the other children.

Dr. MacDowell had wanted to update her on Myrna's

condition. That was all. She wasn't in trouble. She hadn't broken any rules or done anything wrong.

Thank goodness. For a few heart-stopping moments, she'd been afraid Paula had been right, and she'd caused a problem by asking a doctor to check on a patient who wasn't officially his. She only had weeks to go until her insurance coverage as a hospital employee would begin, and heaven knew she needed that insurance. She wasn't ill, except for her annoying allergies, but she'd learned the hard way that living without insurance was risky, indeed.

She'd dropped her car insurance to pay her rent for one month, one lousy month after her previous job had crashed and her roommates had moved out without paying their share. It was perfectly legal in the state of Texas to not carry car insurance. The problem was, shortly after her job crashed, her car had crashed, too. Into a Mercedes-Benz. The judge had ruled her to be at fault, and until she paid for the cost of replacing that Mercedes, her money was not her own. It belonged to the state of Texas, practically every dime of it, thanks to the high monthly payment the judge had set.

The prospect of losing her hospital job was awful on every level, but the idea that she'd be fired just as she was about to have insurance was unbearable. She never wanted to be without insurance—auto, home, medical, dental, *any* insurance—again. The year she'd planned to take off before college had become the year that a lack of insurance had derailed her entire life.

By the time she walked into the playroom, her heart was pounding. Her thoughts were as much to blame as the speed-walking.

Relax. You're not losing your job. Dr. MacDowell is a polite man who knew you'd be curious about Myrna's health, so he filled you in and sat with you for twenty minutes. No big deal.

So why did he want to meet her for lunch tomorrow?

"Hi, guys," Kendry called to a trio of preschoolers as she entered the playroom. Paula sat at the tiny table, monitoring their serious coloring. Since the Myrna Quinones incident, Paula treated Kendry with more courtesy.

It was Sammy, however, who was really happy to see her. He pulled himself to a stand using the bars of his playpen, babbling his baby noises and bouncing in excitement.

"And hello to you, too, my special guy." Kendry scooped him up and gave him a squeeze, just as she caught sight of their reflection in the playroom's window.

"What's up with your dad?" she whispered. She'd never been what her grandfather called "a looker," but the stress of the last few years—the stress she couldn't blame on anyone but herself—had taken its toll.

She rested her cheek on top of Sammy's head. Even in the window's reflection, Sammy's black hair was glossy. Her own hair was a little dull. Her diet was pretty limited while she watched every penny, but she didn't think she was missing that many nutrients, not enough to make her hair less healthy, surely? She'd run out of shampoo and had been making do with bar soap to wash her hair. That probably made it dull, but still clean.

The dark circles under her eyes hadn't gone away in months. Even if she got enough sleep, she had terrible allergies, so the dark circles were here to stay. The bottom line was, she didn't look like the kind of woman a man went out of his way to spend time with.

Whatever lay behind Dr. MacDowell's sudden interest in her was a mystery.

None of it mattered, anyway. Her hair wasn't shiny, but it was clean. Her scrubs were faded, but clean. The important thing was, she was working in a hospital, where she'd always wanted to be. She wasn't a nurse yet, but she had a plan, and the first step had been to become a bona fide employee of the best hospital in Texas. She enjoyed being with the children so much, she might even specialize in pediatric nursing some day.

Sammy grabbed her glasses and succeeded in pulling them off. He chortled in glee. Sammy spent time with her because he liked her.

His father's motives were a mystery.

Be careful what you wish for. You might get it.

How many times had Jamie wished for boredom on the job? While he was deployed, he'd fantasize about what his civilian life would be like. He'd work in an emergency room and treat patients whose medical needs were not truly emergencies, not like the carnage that he'd patched up after firefights. There would be a lot of children with runny noses and slight temperatures, a lot of adults with sprained ankles, and an affluent, overweight businessman getting the wakeup call he needed with a mild first heart attack. For an E.R. doctor, it would be monotony. While in Afghanistan, Jamie had craved monotony.

Now he was getting it. For two weeks, he hadn't had a single challenging case. He told himself that was good.

The E.R. at West Central Hospital had a small locker room for physicians. Off the main E.R. was a kitchenette for the staff, and off the kitchenette was a tiny space euphemistically called the physicians' lounge. It contained a plethora of lab coats, a few metal lockers that no one bothered to put locks on, and a cot that transformed itself from uninviting to nirvana when he had been on his feet for twenty-four hours straight.

At least Sam was happy today. Kendry had been on duty in the playroom, so Jamie could set his worried-parent hat aside for today's shift. She was still far and away Sam's favorite on the list of possible women. In fact, Sam didn't seem to have any particular affinity for any other nurse or medical assistant he came in contact with.

Jamie had made a point of speaking to each woman, anyway. He'd bought one nurse a cup of coffee, shared a slice of cold pizza with another woman while he worked the midnight shift. Quinn had made a point of introducing him to a nurse from the ICU. They were all the same, though, either flirtatious or flustered. The first he had no interest in, the second he had no patience for. He was starting to believe that Kendry Harrison was the only woman in the hospital who could carry on an intelligent conversation without batting her eyelashes.

Jamie half closed the door to the locker room, looking behind it for the dry-cleaning bag that held his white lab coats. Some women entered the kitchenette, and their voices carried into the tiny locker room. "He's a total hottie, even if he seems angry most of the time."

"Hot angry. *Hawt*. Where'd he come from?"

"He's from Dallas, I heard."

"I heard Austin."

"Whatever. He's a Texas boy, coming back after getting out of the army, or some say he's not out yet."

"The army? OMG, imagine him in camouflage and boots. Totally off the hotness scale."

Jamie jerked with surprise. They were talking about him. Had to be. Crap—now he was stuck in here. If he walked out, he'd embarrass the hell out of those women. He crossed his arms and leaned against the lockers. Looked like he was going to stand here and stare at the wall while they made their coffee. He had no choice but to listen to them talk about his *hawt*-ness.

"You didn't see his butt, Terry. He's always in his lab coat."

"I did so see his butt. In the parking lot. No lab coat, just a stethoscope around his neck as he got in his truck."

"Nothing but a stethoscope on? The man drives in the nude?"

Jamie rolled his eyes at the ceiling as the women giggled like girls. Still, it would have been gratifying to have one of his brothers hear him being drooled over. Jamie was the youngest. He was the baby of the three, four years younger than Quinn, six years younger than Braden.

That had been a huge age gap when he'd been in fifth grade while his brothers played high school football. The moms on the football stadium benches had cooed over Jamie, but his brothers had worn helmets and shoulder pads and attracted cheerleaders like flies. Jamie might have been in elementary school, but even then, he'd watched the cheer-leaders in their very short skirts with their very long legs. They'd patted him on the head and watched his brothers.

It was an interesting switch, to be the big man on campus instead of the little brother. Apparently, at this hospital, he was the football star.

"Jamie MacDowell. Scottish sounding. Imagine him in a kilt."

"You're torturing us. It's no use. He's not interested in anybody. Dr. Brown even wore a miniskirt the other day, so it looked like she had nothing on under her lab coat. She looked like a freaking stripper."

"He didn't go for it?"

"Nope. She was pissed. It was one of my more entertain-ing shifts, I'll tell you that."

"Maybe he goes for men."

"I'd bet money he's not gay."

And you'd win. Now, could you ladies—and he mentally snorted in derision at that last word—*now could you ladies take your coffees and go?*

Jamie's cell vibrated silently. He checked the text. Time to get back to work. These women were going to hate him if he walked out of the room now, but the fifth-floor nurse needed alternate pain med orders for a patient he'd admitted.

"The only woman he ever talks to is some homely girl.

I've seen him eat lunch with her in the cafeteria. He doesn't even go in the physicians' lounge. He sits at her table, wherever she is."

"Who? Do we know her?"

"She's nobody. An orderly or something."

They were talking about Kendry, of course. He should have anticipated that sitting with an orderly in the cafeteria would feed the grapevine. This particular grapevine didn't need to be fed further. He already didn't care for the tone of their gossip. Kendry might not be a nurse, but she still contributed to the well-being of this hospital's patients.

"What's this nobody got that Dr. MacDowell likes?"

She's kind. She respects children.

"I can't imagine. She's pitiful-looking. I swear, she wears the same scrubs every day."

"Oh—that girl. I think she decided to make herself over for the new doc. Did you notice she cut her bangs?"

Jamie glared at the door. He'd count to twenty, then he'd leave this little jail cell whether those women were still here or not. He was feeling decidedly less considerate of their feelings.

"Ohmigod, yes. She had to have cut those bangs herself. With children's safety scissors."

"All right, guys, enough. You're being mean to the poor thing," one of the gossiping harpies cut in to defend the absent Kendry—about damned time. Jamie could tell they'd been revving up to pick her to shreds.

"She probably can't afford a decent haircut," the woman defending Kendry said. "She's can't be making more than minimum wage."

"If I made minimum wage, I'd still work a couple hours extra, cut a coupon from the Sunday paper and at least get my hair done at one of those walk-in places. I think she just doesn't care."

"If she didn't care, she wouldn't have cut her bangs at all, would she?"

"Well, of course she cares about Dr. MacDowell. You can't be female and not notice him. Could you imagine them together, though? It'd be like a Greek god and a street urchin in bed."

"You're so mean!"

The nurse made it sound like a compliment.

"Maybe she turns him on, and we can't see why."

Listening to this crap was getting plain painful. True, Kendry didn't turn him on. But she didn't look like a street urchin, for God's sake. She wasn't *homely.* Who gave a damn about her haircut?

"Men have stooped lower. Look at some of the prostitutes we get in the E.R.—I can't believe men pay money to sleep with them. I'd say our soldier-doctor is on a mission to take that orderly on a pity date. Maybe an army buddy dared him to—"

"Yes. Maybe that's why he always looks so angry at the world. He got dared into giving that girl a mercy f—"

The nurses shrieked, literally shrieked, hysterically.

They were comparing Kendry, baby Sam's Kendry, to a prostitute. Jamie used the toe of his cowboy boot to give the door a nudge. It opened slowly as he remained where he was, leaning against the lockers, arms crossed over his chest.

"Oh, crap," said the nurse who saw him first. The other two audibly sucked in their breaths.

"Wanna know why I look so angry all the time, ladies?" Jamie asked in a deliberate, deadly serious drawl.

"Dr. MacDowell, I'm so sorry. I didn't know you—"

"I'm angry that three nurses are taking a break at the same time. That leaves patients lying out there, unattended."

"Yes, sir. We're done now."

Jamie wasn't done with them, however. "I'll tell you what else makes me angry. I'm angry that you'd take time away from patients in order to do nothing except trash a fellow employee at this hospital."

No one said a word to that.

"Her name is Kendry, and she's brilliant with sick kids. Next time you admit a child to the pediatric ward from the E.R., you watch real close if she's the orderly who comes to take them to their room. Watch and learn something about patient care, because she's one of the best we have at West Central. But right now, there are people out there who came to this E.R. for help, so put down your damned coffees and go."

"Sorry."

"Bye."

Jamie didn't move for a moment longer. He was angry, yes. Angry as hell, but also something else, some knot in his chest that made him want to punish something.

Himself.

That was it, damn it, he was mad at himself. For exactly what, he didn't know, but it had something to do with Kendry, with the woman his son loved.

Chapter Five

"Is this seat taken?"

The bass voice sounded soothing in the cacophony of the cafeteria lunch rush. It never failed to send a pleasant shiver down Kendry's back.

"Hi, Dr. MacDowell."

"It's Jamie."

"Hi, Jamie."

The exchange was becoming a little tradition between them. Kendry didn't want to make more of it than it was, but it was nice to have their own private routine, wasn't it?

She smiled at Dr. MacDowell as he sat across from her.

"Soup again?" he asked.

Kendry willed herself to look nonchalant. For whatever reason, *Jamie* treated her like an equal. Like she had brains. Like her opinions mattered. When she spent all day being ordered to change linens and fetch ice, it was a relief to have a man like him to talk to. She wasn't going to shatter the illusion of equality with Jamie by confessing that soup was all she could afford. "Tomato's my favorite. I always get soup when it's tomato."

"I'll have to try it sometime."

The words were bland, ordinary, but he was looking at her…differently.

"Is something wrong?" she asked. Speaking used up air, naturally, so she breathed in again and caught a hint of his aftershave, that delicious, woodsy scent she'd noticed since the first time he'd sat with her.

She snatched a napkin in the nick of time as she turned away and sneezed. At least she'd cut her bangs so she didn't have to push them out of her eyes every time.

"You know," he said, "if I were a doctor, I'd probably give you a diagnosis of allergic rhinitis."

She rolled her eyes at him, but smiled so he'd know she wasn't upset. "I don't think I need to pay for an office visit to find that out."

"I take it that none of the over-the-counter pills are working for you. Do you need a prescription antihistamine?"

"No." Why was he asking about her personal health? They usually talked about other patients' health, not hers.

"I'll write you one." He already had a script pad out of his pocket and was writing away.

"Please, don't bother." She'd never be able to afford it, but she couldn't tell him something so embarrassing.

"It's no problem." He tore off the paper and handed it to her.

"Thanks." She reluctantly took the prescription. Why was he looking at her so strangely? Today's lunch was just…off.

She looked at the paper, so she'd stop trying to analyze his expression. His handwriting was amazingly legible for a doctor, maybe because he wrote in large letters, using up the blank space, filling it with dark ink. No faint scribbles for her to squint at hopelessly. She only had to narrow her eyes a tiny bit to read his writing without her glasses.

This time, when she looked back up at him, he dropped his gaze to his plate. As if she'd caught him in the middle of—something.

"Did you hear something bad today?" she asked.

He looked up at her in surprise, as if she'd guessed right, but he didn't say anything.

"Myrna's not back in dialysis, is she? Or David?"

"No."

She hesitated before a burning need to know made her ask, "It's not about Sam, is it?" Her heart would break if anything happened to that little guy. *Please let it not be something about Sam.*

"No, nothing like that." To her surprise, he reached across the table and squeezed her hand. "Thanks for asking."

She took her hand off the table, grabbed another napkin, turned her head and blew her nose again. It would be nice to sit through a meal with the man without a runny nose.

Because then he'd notice how beautiful you are?

No, but it would be easier to pretend he did.

"I was wondering," Jamie said, "did you get your hair cut?"

"My—what?"

"Did you change your hair?"

"I trimmed my bangs a couple days ago. They were getting in my eyes." She hated this feeling, like she was missing a piece of a puzzle somewhere.

"You look nice."

Good lord, what was going on? Kendry felt herself turn ten shades of red.

Dr. MacDowell nodded once, like that was the end of that subject. Then he picked up his sandwich. "Have you met our new heart patient, little guy named Eric Raines? He came through the E.R. yesterday with a very unusual cardiac rhythm."

Thank goodness the conversation was going back on its

normal track. They usually discussed any kids who had been admitted to the pediatric ward from the emergency room. Dr. MacDowell didn't mind teaching her about all kinds of medical conditions, and she found each one more fascinating than the last. She liked to think he was giving her a mini-internship, a taste of what her final year of nursing school would be like.

"His heart sounds were normal," he said, "but his—"

"Is this seat taken?" asked another deep voice. Without waiting for an answer, a tall man pulled out one of the empty chairs and sat, then leaned his arms on the table. He didn't wear a white lab coat like Jamie, just slacks and a dress shirt with the sleeves cuffed back, but the stethoscope slung around his neck screamed "doctor." He looked from Jamie to Kendry, who summoned a neutral, polite smile.

"Have a seat," Jamie suggested drily.

"Done."

"Kendry, this is my brother Quinn."

She'd already guess that much. The two MacDowell brothers were equally handsome and equally single. Before Jamie had arrived at the hospital, his brother had been the most eligible bachelor. Now there were two bachelors, and the hospital rumor mill had twice as much to speculate about. If she hadn't drawn enough attention to herself by having lunch with Jamie MacDowell, today's lunch with both brothers was sure to do it.

"It's nice to meet you," she said, although she wished everyone in the cafeteria would stop looking over their shoulders at her table.

"Nice to meet you, too." Quinn turned to Jamie. "What kind of abnormal cardiac rhythm patient did you *not* refer to me?"

"Pediatric. Not your specialty. Kendry does a lot of work in the pediatric ward, though." Jamie hesitated, looked at his plate for a moment, then pinned his brother with a firm look. "Kendry is Sam's favorite caregiver in the playroom."

Quinn went utterly still for a second. "I see," he said, turning toward her with much more interest than he'd shown before.

What on earth was going on?

"What do you do here at the hospital, Kendry?" He emphasized her name slightly, like he was making a point of knowing it.

"I'm an orderly." When Quinn raised one eyebrow in unmistakable surprise, she lifted her chin and asked, "What do you do here, Dr. MacDowell?"

His lips twitched at her attempt to sound as condescending as he did. "Mostly, I'm in the cath lab, trying to open up coronary arteries."

"Mostly, he's at his plush private practice," Jamie corrected him. "He only comes to the hospital when he has to do some real work."

"How long have you been an orderly, Kendry?"

She tried to mask her surprise at the question. What was it with MacDowell men asking about her employment background?

"I'm getting close to the six-month mark." And then, because she couldn't help herself, she added, "Why do you ask?"

"Is this your dream job? Or do you have higher aspirations?"

"Quinn, shut up," Jamie said.

Apparently, Dr. Quinn MacDowell thought she was after his brother. A gold digger. Seriously, did she look anything like the kind of woman who attracted rich men?

Any men?

Irritated, she felt compelled to defend herself to the older—and really, much less handsome—Dr. MacDowell.

"For now, this is the best job. I'm working to earn enough

money to get my CMA certification. If the hospital has an opening, then I'll have preferred status as an applicant because I'm already an employee here. The openings are few and far between, so I'm positioning myself to have the best shot at it."

"Your dream job is to be a CMA?" Quinn asked.

"It's a step in the right direction. I'm going to be a nurse. Once I'm a CMA, I'll be able to afford classes toward my bachelor's degree. I can be an RN eight years from now."

Quinn was silent, studying her for a moment. "That sounds like getting your RN the hard way."

"Sometimes that's the only option you have." Kendry toyed with her soup spoon, regretting the words the instant they left her mouth. No one at West Central knew she'd once tried to take the easy way, a year off to play more than work, the year she'd taken the foolish risk of dropping her car insurance. Until she paid off the cost of that accident, she'd do everything the hard way. The right way.

Quinn glanced at Jamie, who was looking at her oddly, then turned back at her. Kendry was definitely missing something.

"I'll tell you what," Quinn said. "When you get that CMA certification, you come see me. I pay more than the hospital does, and I can always use someone with drive and determination. With better pay, you can get that RN degree sooner."

Whatever Kendry had been expecting, it wasn't a job offer. She was certain she blew the good impression she'd apparently made by stumbling over her next words. "Oh. Well. Th-that's very...very—"

"Kendry is interested in pediatrics, not cardiology," Jamie said firmly.

"Well," Quinn drawled, looking at his brother, "since you're in emergency medicine and not pediatrics, you can't make her a better offer, can you?"

Jamie looked like he wanted to punch his brother. Kendry

looked from one to the other, as if she were watching a tennis match. The two Dr. MacDowells were fighting over her? It was insane.

"Maybe I can," Jamie said. "I'll have to see."

Kendry stood up. She nodded at Jamie. "I have to go clock in. Excuse me, Dr. MacDowell." She nodded at Quinn. "Dr. MacDowell." She grabbed her tray and headed for the conveyor belt by the exit.

"What in the hell was that about?" Jamie demanded.

"You can't be serious," Quinn said. "She's got some spunk, no doubt, but she's as plain as can be."

"She's the one who figured out Sam had trouble eating. I still wouldn't have realized he had a cleft palate if it weren't for her."

"Admirable, but not a reason to marry anyone."

"I didn't say I was going to marry her, but she's not plain," Jamie said. "Considering the kind of relationship I want, it wouldn't matter if she were, but I'm sick of hearing people insult her appearance."

"For God's sake, her glasses are held together by tape."

"Kendry is fine the way she is. She's smart. Incredibly smart, and self-taught on medicine like you wouldn't believe. She'll fight for a sick kid with a passion. I've seen her do it."

"For what it's worth, I like her. As an employee. Be rational about this. Hire this Kendry to be the nanny. Hell, I would, after talking to her today."

"I'm not subjecting Sam to another series of nannies. He went through enough of that while I was on active duty. He's going to have a real mother."

Quinn pinched the bridge of his nose and closed his eyes like he was in pain. "When you fall in love and get married, then Sam will have a real mother."

The idea of hiring Kendry as some kind of temporary

mother and then booting her out of the house when another woman came along felt wrong to Jamie on every level.

"What do I tell my son?" Jamie asked. "'Here's someone who loves you and cares for you, but say bye-bye now because I've found someone I want to sleep with'?"

Quinn opened his eyes and leaned forward to speak with forceful quiet. "You can't seriously plan on being celibate the rest of your life. You might be in mourning for your baby's mother right now, but one day you won't want to be buried anymore. You'll look around and what will you see?"

Quinn gestured toward the empty chair. "You're going to be tied to this…this…*girl,* and it will cost you half of everything you own to get the divorce you need, unless you have an ironclad prenup."

Jamie stood up, angry—the same kind of anger he'd felt when the nurses had cut Kendry to shreds.

He left the cafeteria through its outdoor dining area, planning to take a shortcut to the emergency room through the hospital's parklike courtyard. Quinn dogged his every step, still talking.

Jamie tuned him out. He didn't need legal protection against Kendry. Whomever he married would be providing *him* protection if the State Department should attempt to remove Sam from his custody. Removing a child from a stable, two-parent home would look bad. Jamie could leverage that in the press, if he had to.

If the State Department investigated. They might, because no child had been brought to the States from Afghanistan by an American soldier. He'd checked. No Afghani child had been adopted by a non-Muslim, period, just as no soldier had been granted permission to marry an Afghani.

If Sam wasn't his biological child. He might not be, because Amina had told him that life was short, that she lived to seize the day because you never knew when someone you loved might die. The rumor mill said there'd been someone she'd loved before she loved Jamie, someone who'd been killed in action.

If. Always *if* hanging over his head, a sword that, if it fell, could cut Sam out of his life.

"How do you plan on going from lunches with an orderly who calls you 'Dr. MacDowell' to proposing marriage?"

"Hell, Quinn, I don't have all the answers. I only know that Sam is attached to Kendry. She's pleasant, she's intelligent, and she seems to be attached to Sam, too. So, yeah, I'm having lunch with her every day."

An image flashed in his mind of Kendry in his house. He could see her holding Sam, standing in the kitchen, smiling the way she did when she talked about life with her unconventional parents. Jamie would not be alone. Someone would share his burdens.

"She'd be the one doing me the favor if she married me," Jamie said, stopping by a sumac tree.

Quinn was silent.

The leaves of the sumac were already starting to turn orange for fall. Less than two weeks were left before he reported to his new reserve unit for the first weekend drill. Sam was scheduled for his palate repair after that. Once that was healed, the hole in the wall of his heart would be repaired. Now that Sam was nearing his first birthday, the surgeons were willing to fix the things he'd been too frail to address earlier in his life.

Jamie rubbed his jaw, too tired to fight, too weary to explain.

Quinn filled the silence. "Kendry is the one, then?"

The world stopped. For a moment, everything was suspended. Slowly, Jamie turned his gaze from the orange leaves to meet his brother's eyes.

"Yes, she is."

Quinn shook his head. "Then I can't believe I'm saying this, but good luck."

Jamie walked the rest of the way to the emergency room before he remembered something important.

Amina.

He'd thought he'd marry Amina. Instead, he'd returned to the States with her child. *Their* child. Now he had to figure out how to ask a near stranger named Kendry to marry him, because Amina's child loved her, even if Jamie never would.

Chapter Six

"You are my favorite guy in the whole, wide world."

Kendry sat on the playroom floor and crooned sweet nothings to Sammy as he lay on his back on a blanket. Holding his little baby feet in her hands, she moved his legs like he was riding a bike.

"Where's that big, baby laugh?" She wiggled his feet. "I wanna hear that baby laugh."

Sam gifted her with his wide-open, mostly toothless smile.

"That's my guy!"

She loved this kind of day, when she was the only adult in the playroom and could lavish her attention on the children without feeling self-conscious. Sammy made her feel like a superstar. Everything she said was apparently what his little baby ears wanted to hear.

She stretched out on her side next to Sammy, propping her head up with one hand and tickling the baby's belly with her other. "Let's do this for a living. Forget all this bill-paying college stuff. We'll lie on a beach all day in Guatemala, like my parents."

Sammy cooed at her and grabbed his own toes.

"You're right. You need to live here. Stay in school, kid. It's harder than it looks to make ends meet without a degree."

She'd done some hard labor after work the previous evening, swinging at waist-high weeds with a machete, of all things. The house across the street from her rented room had been foreclosed on, and the bank was trying to clean up the yard a bit before its auction. She'd earned twenty dollars, cash, by helping the yard crew for only two hours, sneezing all the way.

Now, however, she was paying a price in aching arm muscles. She flopped onto her belly on the cushy mat. She was horizontal, the playroom was quiet, and the cutest baby in town was lying safely next to her, as content and happy as he could be. If she wasn't careful, she would drift off to sleep.

Sam grabbed a fistful of her ponytail and yanked.

"Ow! I'm awake, Sammy. I swear."

"That's not how it looked to me," his father drawled.

"Eek!" Kendry pressed her hand on her chest as her heart skipped a beat.

"Didn't mean to scare you. Sam saw me coming and tried to warn you."

Kendry gave Sammy's belly a jiggle. "That's 'cause you're on my team, aren't you?"

When she moved to get to her feet, she nearly collided with Jamie, who was hunkering down on his heels to greet his son. The man was just so big. Not only tall, but wide in the shoulders, like he'd played football or something. This close, she could feel the warmth of him, smell his skin, and—

"Ah-choo!" Kendry barely turned her head in time to sneeze into her elbow.

"Did you get that antihistamine prescription filled yesterday?"

"Not yet." *Not ever.*

"You'd feel a lot better."

Not if Mrs. Haines kicked me out of her garage for not paying this week's rent, I wouldn't. I'm not going back to the homeless scene, not even for you.

Dr. MacDowell stood and looked down at her, frowning. "It's been a week since Sam broke those glasses."

Kendry picked up Sam and stood, too. "They're still wearable. Why get new ones if a toddler's going to whack them?" She grabbed the earpiece—the one without the bandage tape—and wiggled the glasses up and down, doing her eyebrows, too, like Groucho Marx. "These are now my special Sammy glasses."

Usually, Dr. MacDowell laughed at the jokes she made. They were the best way to deflect any comments that might lead to a more revealing conversation than she was willing to have. This time, he only smiled faintly. "But you did get new glasses? My offer to pay for them stands. My son broke them, so it seems only fair."

She waved a hand in the air breezily and hiked Sam up a little higher on her hip. "I'll get new ones. I've been busy. These aren't dead yet, anyway." It was time for a change of subject. "I've been reading up on cleft-palate repairs, so I'll know what to expect when Sam is with me afterward."

She had a hard time remembering the questions she'd wanted to ask about the surgery's recovery stages, because while she held Sam on her hip, Jamie started patting him on his back. The move made the three of them seem connected. It was intimate. It was unnerving.

As Kendry stumbled over her question, Sam squealed and grabbed her glasses. Thankful for the excuse to break the moment, Kendry laughed. "See? Sammy glasses."

"I see." He righted the glasses on her nose, and then Jamie

MacDowell, M.D., the most eligible bachelor at West Central Hospital—the most eligible bachelor in Texas, she'd bet—smoothed a piece of her hair behind her ear, let his hand drift to her shoulder, and looked deeply into her eyes.

For that moment, the fantasy was real. Jamie was interested in her. Interested in *that* way.

Kendry dropped her gaze. *Too, too real.*

He squeezed her shoulder gently. "Some parents don't pay as much attention to their own children as you do to Sam."

This brought her gaze back to him. So that's what this was all about. He was warning her that she was too attached to a child that wasn't hers. She'd dealt with this kind of parent before.

"You're number one in Sam's world," she said. "Just because he likes me, that doesn't mean he doesn't love you."

The playroom door opened and her replacement came in, a CMA named Bailey who was wonderfully friendly to all— even orderlies. "Good evening, Dr. MacDowell. Hi, Kendry."

Kendry pushed Sam into Jamie's arms, turned away and sneezed. "Excuse me." She put a lot of distance between them, walking to the hand sanitizer dispenser and squirting the cold foam into her hand.

Jamie followed her, standing a tiny bit too close. "I meant that as a compliment. If I have to be at work, then I want Sam to be with someone he likes." His words were quiet and low, meant for her ears only.

She tried not to shiver at the goose bumps he raised. "Some parents don't feel that way. I've had at least one staff member who was jealous that her daughter would cling to me when she came to pick her up in the afternoons. That little girl doesn't come to the hospital's day-care center anymore."

"You're kidding."

"It's tough, sometimes. I thought that baby was a real sweetie, and now I'll never see her again."

"You'd rather stay with the same kid, year after year?"

There it was again, that intense look in his eyes. Kendry tried to deflect the question away from herself.

"Not just any kid," she said. Hoping to lighten the mood, she threw a comically exaggerated look over her shoulder, as if Bailey might hear something scandalous. "Let's be honest. Some of them can be a real pain. Not everyone was born as charming as your Sam."

"Our Sam."

"What?"

Jamie looked away. She watched him swallow nervously. *Nervously?*

"I meant," he began, speaking carefully, "that Sam seems to be as happy with you as he is with me." With a glance in Bailey's direction, he leaned near to Kendry's ear. "And I think that's very, very important."

Kendry had stopped rubbing the foam into her hands. That low voice drawling in her ear was...upsetting.

She tried to rub the sticky remains briskly into her palms as she headed for the crib where Sam had taken his nap. She picked up the denim diaper bag and turned toward Jamie, sticking her arm straight out to hand it to him from the great distance of her arm's length. Her tired muscles protested.

"Will you be back tomorrow?" Kendry asked.

Jamie took the bag from her without a trace of nervousness. Instead, he winked. "You couldn't keep us away."

As he left with Sammy, Bailey whistled quietly. "How did you do that?"

"Do what?"

"Get dreamy Dr. MacDowell interested in you."

"In me? You must be crazy."

"Did you not see the way that man smiled at you? I didn't know he had a dimple. Ye gods, if that man smiled more often, every woman in this town would come up with some reason to go to the emergency room."

Kendry hadn't known he had a dimple, either. But, *oh my,* he most certainly did, on the right side.

"Sit down here and tell me everything." Bailey settled into one of the two rocking chairs.

Kendry needed to sit down. "There's nothing to tell."

"Has he asked you out?"

"Be serious. Look at him. Look at me."

"Well…I don't know…" Bailey's certainty faded.

Kendry's certainty grew, the certainty that reading anything more into Jamie's smile tonight was foolish.

"He's happy that Sam is doing so well now that he's eating sitting up."

Bailey accepted her explanation, but as Kendry closed her eyes and rocked, she saw Jamie MacDowell's smile.

I wish we were more than friends.

She stopped rocking. The truth of that wish was powerful. Dangerous.

It was better to have Jamie MacDowell as a friend than nothing at all, just as it was better to be an orderly in a hospital than not work in medicine at all. Just as it was better to live in a converted garage than in a homeless shelter. Just as—

When had her life become a series of compromises?

When you wished for more than you had, and you ended up with nothing.

Wishes could be dangerous, indeed. If she wished for more than she had with Jamie MacDowell, she'd only raise hopes that would be dashed. She would end up not just broke, but brokenhearted.

That was too high a price to pay for any wish.

Chapter Seven

"Damn it, get me a nurse!"

Jamie had thought his wish for a boring job had been granted, but it was one of those days in the E.R., the kind when a multicar accident and staffing cuts combined to make every moment a crisis.

"There are no more nurses, Dr. MacDowell. Everyone's tied up." His nurse sounded frantic, lying as she was on the patient's legs, trying to keep the half-conscious man from doing greater harm to himself.

Jamie kept his eyes on the gash in the patient's side, his hand pressing the severed vein shut, his other hand keeping the retractor in place. "An MA, then. An orderly. Anyone with two hands."

"How can I help?"

He recognized Kendry's voice immediately.

"They sent me down from peds," she said breathlessly, as if she'd been running, "and another orderly is on his way from ortho. I'm supposed to tell you the on-call doctor will be here in thirty."

Jamie didn't take his eyes off the vein. "Get this patient's oxygen back in place."

"Okay, it's on."

"Switch places with the nurse. Don't let those legs move." To the nurse, he gave orders for deeper sedation. He and Kendry held their positions until the patient went under. "Kendry, turn that suction on and get me a second laceration tray."

The tension in the back of Jamie's neck lessoned a fraction. He could work with Kendry—and work they did. He barked orders, and she responded quickly. The nurse assisted him with the emergency surgery, but it was Kendry who made that possible by knowing where to find everything he needed, from surgical instruments to saline. When the patient was stabilized, it was Kendry who hand-carried Jamie's notes as she rolled the patient's bed to the regular operating room, where surgeons had been called in to take over the rest of the patient's care.

Hours passed as patient after patient made their way through the emergency room. Sometimes Kendry was with him, sometimes a different member of the staff. Every bed in the E.R. was full, from the privately walled cubicles to the spillover area, where beds were only separated by curtains. The waiting room was packed, several nurses had told him.

Jamie had signed a half-dozen discharge orders, but patients still occupied beds, waiting for their transportation either to regular hospital rooms or to the exit, whichever Jamie had decided was appropriate.

"Orderly!" Jamie barked at a very young man who was standing still in the middle of the rush. "I'm waiting on these beds to open up. Where's the wheelchair I asked for?"

"There aren't any more around." He fluttered his hands, helpless.

"Then go find one. Now. I want these rooms turned over."

Kendry passed Jamie at a half-jog, snagging the orderly's arm as she went. "Come on. You have to go to the parking lot and get the wheelchairs." Jamie caught her eye, and she made a face that clearly said, *Where do they hire these people?*

Jamie smiled to himself as he entered the next cubicle. Kendry could read his mind. Being married to her would be easy.

The rain that had caused the night's car accidents hadn't let up. Neither had the volume of patients. Kendry had learned more during this shift than she'd dreamed possible. No wonder nurses and doctors had extensive internships. There was nothing like being on the scene, and tonight, the E.R. was like a scene from a TV show, intense and dramatic. Every time the glass double doors to the ambulance ramp slid open, the damp night air whooshed in with another patient.

One stretcher had been wheeled into a cubicle by two paramedics while a third paramedic straddled the patient, pumping hard with two hands on the prone man's chest. While Kendry had replenished oxygen masks and blankets across the hall, she'd heard Jamie's calm command, "Clear," before the unmistakable sound of defibrillator paddles. It was dizzying to realize that a life was being saved just feet away from her.

She often heard Jamie call her by name. "Kendry, grab a lumbar-puncture tray and meet me in room three." She'd learned about the importance of the bevel on the needle and how the manometer worked, even as she'd smiled for the woman getting the spinal tap and tucked a warm blanket over her shoulders to counter the cold of her exposed lower back.

She'd had to gown up in protective gear in order to peel the mask, gown and gloves off Jamie after he'd stabilized a bloody patient. "You keep that gear on while you clean this room," Jamie had said to her sternly as he'd left her for the next patient, instructions that weren't necessary, but that made her feel like he was watching out for her.

Always, when a child was involved, his tone was softer. She learned that he called the little girls "princess," every one of them. "Okay, princess, I brought you someone special. This is Kendry, and she's going to take you and your mommy to get a picture of your arm. Your mom can climb on board and Kendry will push your whole bed. You have to be in a hospital to get a cool ride like that."

Then suddenly, the pace slowed. Kendry stood near the central nurses' station and checked off each room in her mind. Each one was occupied, but not one case was critical. Most patients were in a holding pattern until test results came in. Jamie was standing at the nurses' station, updating chart after chart. If she had been half in love with him before, she was a goner now. The man was the real deal: handsome, skilled, calm in a storm.

Kendry glanced at the clock. Six hours. She hadn't stopped running for six hours. She'd been called down from the pediatric ward only after the E.R. had been swamped for some time. That meant Jamie had been running even longer than she had. The decisions he'd been making, the responsibility on his shoulders—shoulders which, even now, looked strong enough to carry them and more—

Yes, she was a goner.

Who watched out for him? Shouldn't the leader be taken care of, so he could take care of everything else? With that thought in mind, she took a Popsicle and a carton of milk from the supply kept for patients, then returned to the nurses' station. She waited patiently while Jamie dictated notes into the hospital phone.

He noticed her immediately, finished speaking into the phone while he kept his eyes on her, and hung up. "What's up?"

She held up the Popsicle and the milk carton. "Which do you need more? Sugar or protein?"

He shook his head and smiled with that one-sided dimple. "I'll take both. You are my favorite person in this entire hospital."

She nearly blushed. "Nah. Sam's upstairs, remember? He's sleeping. I peeked in on my way back down from ortho."

"Did you?" His smile started to fade, although he didn't look angry or upset. Just…intense. Again. He told the nurses he was going on break. "Take a walk with me?" he asked Kendry.

"Sure."

He led the way outside the sliding glass doors to the ambulance ramp, where an admin clerk was startled in the middle of a forbidden cigarette. The entire hospital grounds were designated as a no-smoking area, but with the pouring rain, no one wanted to cross the street for their smoke break. The covered portico had sheltered more than a few smokers tonight.

"Sorry, Dr. MacDowell," the clerk said, quickly crushing out her cigarette. She narrowed her eyes at Kendry, looked between her and Jamie, and shook her head slightly. "See you inside in a few."

Jamie sat on a metal bench and gestured for Kendry to sit beside him. "Tired?" he asked.

"I'm afraid I will be if I stop moving. This has been crazy, but time sure flies when it's this busy. Getting six hours of overtime isn't bad, either."

"It isn't always this busy. It's amazing how a hard rain guarantees a car accident or two, every time."

"Do you like it when it's busy?"

"That's a trick question. How can I say I enjoy seeing people in pain and need?" Jamie crunched the last mouthful of Popsicle off the wooden stick. "I'll tell you the truth.

If the intensity of the rush didn't make me feel alive, then I wouldn't be an emergency physician. People either welcome that adrenaline, or they don't. The ones that don't shouldn't choose this specialty."

He downed the milk in a few gulps. With his head thrown back and the carton at his lips, his thirst seemed almost carnal to Kendry. She watched him, feeling that schoolgirl crush mature into something more physical.

And equally hopeless. Be happy that he's your friend. Don't wish for more.

Without standing, Jamie pitched the empty carton and the naked Popsicle stick into the nearest trash can. Then he angled himself toward her, stretching his arm across the back of the bench. "How about you? Would you like to be an E.R. doctor after tonight?"

"I really want to be a nurse. I'm more about the patient care than I am about the diagnosing."

"Would you want to be an E.R. nurse, then?"

Kendry turned away to better see the rain coming down beyond the overhang. Better to keep a few inches between her back and his hand. "I have a long time left to decide." She ducked her chin a bit, then slid him a glance. With a grin, she confessed, "But I was kind of loving that adrenaline in there tonight."

Jamie laughed. "I knew you were. You're either cut out for it or you're not. You've got what it takes."

His praise made Kendry want to burst with pride, but she tried to play it casual, crossing her arms over her chest and shrugging. "I've also got what it takes to fall asleep on a playroom floor with your son."

"I've got that, too."

They both laughed, and then Jamie placed his warm hand very firmly on her shoulder. This was no casual brushing of body parts. He was touching her on purpose, laughing with her.

Don't wish for more.

"Kendry, don't you see it? What a good pair we are?"

"We…" The sound of the rain was nearly drowned out by the sudden buzzing in her head. "We are?"

"In the middle of all this adrenaline, you stopped and checked on Sam, too. He's on your mind, like he's always on mine."

"I wanted… It was just a habit, really. I see him almost every day, so…"

"You're the closest thing to a mother he's got."

"I am?"

Jamie tightened his grip on her shoulder. "Kendry, listen to me. You can skip the CMA thing and go straight to nursing school. You should be a nurse. You have amazing instincts when it comes to patients."

The rain kept falling, and Kendry kept feeling lost by the conversation. "Are you—are you offering me a scholarship?"

"I have enough money for anything you need. Tuition, books." He paused and flicked a glance at the bandage that kept the earpiece of her eyeglasses together. "Glasses."

"I never heard of a scholarship that included glasses."

"I'm not talking about a scholarship."

"Then what are you—"

"Marry me."

For one second, Kendry was shocked. The next, she was hurt. Jamie didn't know what he was playing with. He couldn't know how hard she was working toward that nursing degree. Still, to joke about marrying someone was odd. "You had me going there for a minute. I thought you were serious about the nursing school."

"I've never been more serious. Marry me, and my money becomes our money. And our money can certainly be spent on your education."

"Marriage? We're barely friends."

"We're definitely friends."

"But—" She groped for the right thing to say. What she was hearing was so far from what she could possibly have expected. "You don't marry someone because you're friends."

"You are more than just a friend to me, Kendry."

She swallowed hard. She'd wished he saw her as more than a friend, and now here he was, about to tell her that her wish had come true. It didn't seem right. It didn't seem possible.

"This is an awfully big leap," she whispered, "from friends to marriage. You've never taken me on a date. We've never kissed."

At that, he seemed almost surprised. He let go of her shoulder and brought his hand to the back of his neck, kneading the muscles there in something of a nervous gesture. "I wasn't thinking of that kind of marriage."

"I see." She saw nothing. What other kind of marriage was there?

"I want a wife who'll be my partner raising Sam. I want my marriage to complete my family. I didn't mean that I wanted something, uh, romantic." He gestured between them with his hand. "We don't have that kind of thing. You know that."

No kind of chemistry between them? It was nothing more than she'd expected, that Jamie didn't see her as girlfriend material, let alone wife material. He said it bluntly, in a tone that made it seem like he was stating something obvious. She felt sick to her stomach.

Jamie ducked his head a little, looking at her face, not letting her break eye contact. He chuckled. "I've sprung this on you a little too suddenly, huh? I'm not doing this very well."

Jamie picked up one of her hands in his. "I didn't plan on asking you here, but didn't tonight prove how well we work together? You're perfect for the kind of marriage I'm offering. The fact that we get along so well is an incredible bonus, as far as I'm concerned, because the most important thing is that Sam loves you."

Kendry looked down at their loosely joined hands. Jamie ducked down to make eye contact again. "Sam does love you. There's no doubt of that."

Two women came from around the corner. They must have been outside for a smoke break, standing around the corner this whole time. They'd barely passed Kendry when they made those horrible sounds people make when they are trying to hold their laughter in.

The rain had stopped. Kendry hadn't noticed it stopping, but the silence was now oppressive. "You keep bringing up Sam. How about Sam's mother?" she said, jerking her hand away. "Maybe she'd like to fill the role."

"She died during his birth." Jamie let her hand go. "I thought you knew."

Poor Sam. Now her heart hurt along with her stomach for poor little Sammy, and the poor woman who had never had the chance to cuddle her baby. Jamie was trying to fill the hole that woman must have left. Not the emptiness she'd apparently left in his heart, though. Only the empty space where a mother for Sam should be.

Or maybe her heart hurt because she felt sorry for herself. Poor little Kendry, so undesirable that a man thought she'd marry him without a kiss.

She stood up, which seem to startle Jamie, because he stood up, too, and stepped closer to her. "Do you need some time, maybe? Do you…do you want to talk about it?"

"No, I understand everything now. The lunches, meeting your brother, the way you kept asking for me tonight whenever the patient was a child. It was all an audition. You've been looking for a woman who would agree to a loveless marriage, and you think I'm that woman."

"Not loveless. I want Sam to be raised in a home where his parents love him madly. Both of them."

A *sexless* marriage. That's what she didn't have the guts to say. She was the perfect woman that an intelligent, caring man like Jamie MacDowell thought would jump at the chance for a sexless marriage.

No other man has made you any offer at all. Have you looked in a mirror?

The glass doors slid open and stayed open as some paramedics strolled out with an empty stretcher. Kendry didn't want to speak in front of any more witnesses. Heck, she didn't want to speak ever again. She didn't want to be here.

But she and Jamie stayed where they were, silent, until the sounds inside the emergency room reached her ears. Snatches of voices. "I swear on a stack of Bibles. He asked her to marry him." Snippets of conversation. "Not that kind of marriage." Shrieks of laughter.

This was it. This was the price she'd now pay for reaching above herself and imagining that she was someone besides the girl who counted pennies. She'd had a grand future planned for herself at West Central Hospital. Now she wouldn't be able to hold her head up.

"It doesn't matter what other people think," Jamie said stiffly. He must have heard every word she had. "If our arrangement works for us, who cares?"

"I care. I care that everyone in this hospital thinks I'm a joke. I thought you were my friend. You're not."

"Kendry." He reached out to touch her arm, but she backed up.

"I have to go clock out now. Goodbye, Dr. MacDowell."

With her head held high, Kendry walked through the E.R. to the bank of elevators. She hoped her broken glasses hid the tears in her eyes.

Chapter Eight

Where the hell was Kendry?

Two nights ago, she'd clearly been upset when she'd left the E.R. The patient load had prevented him from following her, but he'd told himself it was okay. They were okay. After all, the gossip had hurt her feelings, but Jamie had only said nice things to her about how much he wanted her in his life. She couldn't have meant it when she said he wasn't her friend.

When he'd brought Sam to the playroom on his next shift, a medical assistant he didn't know had told him that Kendry was already gone for the day. Kendry normally worked the day shift, but Jamie had taken the swing shift; that was why their paths hadn't crossed.

Today, he was back on the day shift. He'd been counting on finding Kendry in the playroom. Sam fussed when Jamie left him with a stranger.

The playroom had been full, as it usually was in the mornings. The two women on duty were not Kendry, however. Sam had cried when Jamie left him, which always tore at his nerves. He was determined to find Kendry in the cafeteria at lunch.

So where was she? He stood in the center of the dining area and turned in a slow circle, ignoring everyone who watched him. He checked the line of people waiting for the cashier. Nothing.

They'd met for lunch every time they'd both been working at the hospital. Every single day for nearly a month. She had to know he'd be looking for her, so why was she being so hard to find?

She has no reason to avoid me. I told her she was perfect for me. I told her my son loved her. I promised to send her to nursing school. I proposed to her.

But she hadn't said yes. She'd been embarrassed by some gossip and had taken off running. She couldn't blame him for that, could she?

Apparently, she could.

Okay, so his proposal had been clumsy, and it hadn't occurred to him to sweep the area for eavesdroppers, but that wasn't a good reason for her to avoid him now. His relationship with Kendry was better than that. Without any romantic ties, they could just be friends. Friends didn't avoid each other.

By the time Jamie found her in the courtyard, he was feeling decidedly unfriendly. He'd walked past her twice without seeing her. For one thing, she had her back to the cafeteria and was seated on the farthest possible park bench. For another, she was wearing bright pink. He'd been looking for traditional green scrubs, the kind she always wore.

But it was Kendry, all right, taped glasses in place, mopping her nose with a fistful of napkins, as usual. "There you are," he said, not attempting to keep the accusation from his tone.

She jumped like a startled bird and blinked up at him

from under her bangs. She hadn't been sneezing, he realized. She'd been crying. Was still crying.

All his anger and irritation fled in an instant. "Kendry, what's wrong?"

She hid her face in her napkin immediately and shooed him away with one hand.

Right. Like he'd leave his friend like this. Jamie sat on the bench. Kendry scooted a few inches away from him. With each snuffled breath, her shoulders shook a little bit. Helplessly, he waited while she caught her breath, watched as she trembled in her stiff clothes.

She looked frail. He'd known she was thin, of course, but the pink scrubs emphasized how thin. They were obviously new, still creased from their packaging. He wished she'd say something. He wanted to help; her tears were distressing.

Of course they were. Tears pretty much equaled distress, but Kendry's tears seemed somehow worse to him. Maybe because she was usually so sharp, so enthusiastic about her job. About Sam. About life.

He patted her on the shoulder, lightly, the way he patted Sam when he needed soothing.

"I'm sorry," she finally said, pushing her bangs aside with the back of one hand. "I didn't think anyone would find me here."

"You did make it a challenge. I've been looking for a while. What's wrong?"

"Nothing, really. Just having a pity party."

She wasn't going to say any more, he could tell. She threw the last bit of a saltine at the base of a tree, for the squirrels or birds or ants.

"What's the occasion, then, for the pity party?"

"Oh—" She flicked the back of her hand toward the tree, a sign of general irritation with the air. "It's nothing."

Jamie felt a little irritated himself. In his experience, women didn't cry over nothing, despite popular male opinion to the contrary. But also in his experience, if a man asked what was wrong and then sat patiently and asked a second time—not that he thought he deserved a medal for it or anything—then the woman would be glad to share her reasons for crying.

Not Kendry. She crumpled the cellophane cracker wrapper in her fist and sat there, napkin in one hand and wrapper in the other.

Was he supposed to ask a third time?

He looked from her clenched fists to her face. She was looking away from him, which allowed him to study her profile. Her glasses were halfway down her wet nose, so he could see that no fresh tears were falling from her mostly green eyes, but her lashes were wet.

Really thick lashes.

Really irrelevant thought. The important thing was, she was upset, and she wouldn't explain why. His eyes dropped to her mouth, as if he'd find a reason why words were failing to appear there. Her lips were pressed together, hard, with a tremor. She didn't want to cry around him.

Whose shoulder did she cry on, then? Frankly, he didn't like the idea that there might be someone else she felt more comfortable with. The background check he'd ordered on her had come back clean. No criminal past, only a single court appearance for a traffic accident. She'd earned a GED after sporadic school attendance, which Jamie knew was due to her parents' travels. She'd never been married, and there was no indication that she had any man in her life, or that she did much besides work and go home to someplace she rented, for no property was in her name.

In other words, Kendry had no other person's shoulder to cry on.

And so, for a third time, he asked her.

"Kendry, what's wrong?"

* * *

The man was persistent. In a good way, if she were honest with herself. Persistent like a friend would be.

She sniffed in the last of her teary, sloppy self. Blew her breath upward to puff her bangs out of her eyes and tipped her head back to look at the sky. It was crisscrossed with the branches of the sumac tree. Very pretty. Picturesque.

"Nothing's really wrong. I got thrown up on by one of the kids in the playroom. I had to get these new scrubs."

"I know you can handle the sight of blood, but vomit can be something else entirely, can't it?"

I'm not going to cry. I'm not going to cry. No matter how nice he is to me, I'm not going to cry.

Jamie kept being nice. "I'd understand if it grossed you out to be thrown up on, but why the tears?" He was trying to make her smile. Her heart broke a little more. Could she have dreamed up a more perfect man? Too bad she was barely even a female to him. He'd made that clear.

I didn't mean that I wanted something romantic. We don't have that kind of thing. You know that.

She looked down at the too-sharp crease in the too-crisp pants. "They made me take these scrubs. I didn't want them."

"Why not? You don't like the color? C'mon, Kendry, talk to me. Something's gotten to you, bad."

"These are too expensive." She said it very quietly as she used the index finger of one hand to trace the crease. Cracker crumbs from the cellophane in her palm left a little trail. "It's my fault. I should have had a spare set on hand, but I didn't, so my supervisor ordered me to put these on."

"Ordered you to buy scrubs? They could have loaned you a set. The E.R. has stacks of them."

"For their department. Departments don't share that much, you know. All we have at peds is a supply of tiny gowns that don't close in the back." She spared him a quick glance. "Seriously, you don't realize how easy it is to ask for something when you're a doctor. I can't pick up the phone and call surgery or emergency and ask them to send me a pair of scrubs."

"Your supervisor could have called."

Fresh tears sprang to her eyes. Tears of frustration, this time. "You have no idea what life is like at the bottom of the totem pole, Dr. MacDowell."

"It's Jamie, remember?"

He shifted closer to her, studying her. Kendry regretted her words already, and the scrutiny they were causing. She had her pride. It would be awful for him to know how tempting his offer of marriage had been from a purely financial standpoint.

"Call me next time," he said, "but if I know you, you'll always have a spare set on hand now."

"I only have one set, if you haven't noticed."

"No, I didn't."

That almost made her smile. "Typical man."

"All scrubs look alike," he countered.

And you don't notice my appearance.

"My supervisor said I needed a second pair, anyway. I do wash my scrubs, you know, every single night. They're clean."

It was such a struggle, day after day, getting those scrubs in the sink, working the soap in, rinsing and rinsing and rinsing until the suds all came out. Hanging them up so they'd be dry by her next shift. It was a daily necessity, and she hadn't failed, not one day, to get it done. She greeted her children in clean clothes every morning.

She shifted in the scratchy new scrubs.

"Of course they're clean," Jamie said, and she could practically hear the frown in his voice.

"Thank you." Kendry sniffed again, sucking the tears back in an unladylike fashion, but she refused to weep anymore. "But my supervisor doesn't think it's possible for a person to wash her scrubs every single day, I guess."

She looked at Jamie fully for the first time since he'd sat down. The concern in his expression just about made the weeping start again, so she went back to looking up at the tree, focusing on the beauty of the branches against the sky. "It's okay. They'll dock my pay a little every week for the next eight weeks. I can survive eight weeks."

Desperation—fear—crawled up her throat a little bit, but she pushed it back down. She'd been told to clock out early today. Those extra six hours at the E.R. couldn't be paid as overtime after all, so she had to go home to prevent her time sheet from going over its weekly forty hours.

Still, even with her pay being docked for the cost of these scrubs, she'd pay the rent. That was most important, not to end up on a sidewalk, unprotected. Not to go backward, back to the homeless shelter.

She was so busy coming up with a new budget for the next eight weeks that Jamie caught her utterly, completely by surprise when he cupped her cheek in his hand and turned her to face him.

Her first thought was *his hand is so warm*.

Then, *his hand is so large*.

And as her eyes closed, so she wouldn't have to look into his and their unbearable concern, she thought, *his hand is so gentle*.

It was her undoing. Tears ran down her cheeks, no matter how hard she scrunched her eyes shut, but Jamie's warm, large, gentle hand drew her head to his shoulder. She leaned her forehead against the smooth cotton of his dress shirt, pressed her face into the male muscle underneath and sobbed.

Her careful plans had come undone. She'd nearly had enough saved to take the last course to become a certified medical assistant. Nearly. She thought longingly of the envelope labeled *school* that she had taped to the inside of her dresser drawer. She'd been managing to put five dollars in it, every week, on a schedule to start classes in February.

For the next eight weeks, though, her paycheck was going to get docked. She quickly did the math in her head, something she'd gotten good at. Her rent was an even one hundred dollars per week. These scrubs, with their contrast piping, were fifty dollars. Six dollars and twenty-five cents would be missing from her paycheck every week. There went the five dollars for tuition, plus another dollar and twenty-five cents that would have to come out of which envelope?

Food. There was no other choice. The court-ordered payment took more than half of her paycheck, but it was not negotiable.

She gulped and hiccupped, but couldn't stop a fresh waterfall of tears. Jamie's shirt was going to get soaked, but the weight of his hand was keeping her head on his shoulder.

She had to keep the tuition money. She had to. She'd never get out of debt if she didn't have the qualification for a better-paying position.

She could keep the five dollars for her tuition if she skipped lunch three or four days each week, but lunch was all she had. She always saved her plastic bowl and refilled it before leaving her shift, getting two meals for the price of one. Although Kendry had learned that she didn't need to eat much, even she couldn't get by without three days of meals.

Maybe she could drink the juice and eat the Popsicles that were kept on hand for the patients. Her conscience objected, though. She felt guilty enough today for eating the crackers that came with the soup when she hadn't bought soup. She could go without food one or two days a week, couldn't she?

Probably not. She would have to delay her classes. Again.

"I'll be okay," she said out loud. For Jamie's benefit, and her own. There was no law that said she had to start the CMA class in February. June would be here before she knew it.

She lifted her head, but Jamie pressed her back down into his shoulder and put his arm around her. "Be still for a moment," he said. "Relax."

Relax? She almost laughed. First, she was too anxious about money to relax. On top of that, Jamie was too damned handsome for a woman to think of relaxing in his embrace—and no matter how he viewed her, she was quite aware that she was a woman whenever he was near. He smelled good, warm and woodsy, and the shoulder she rested her forehead on was all muscle. It would be terribly easy to turn her face toward his throat and taste his skin. Since kissing him was out of the question—and would result in a humiliating scene for her—she faked relaxation as best she could.

Mostly, she wanted to run away from this man who was everything she wasn't.

"Don't let this supervisor get to you," Jamie said, his breath warm on her hair. "It sounds like she threw her authority around a little, but it's only a set of scrubs."

He thought her feelings were hurt, then? He thought this was an issue of pride?

Her own conscience prodded her: *Isn't it?* She was too proud to admit how poor she was, how far in debt she'd dug herself. The hole had been of her own doing; it was up to her to dig her way back out. Jamie was right. She was too proud to tell her supervisor why she couldn't afford the scrubs.

"Let things like that roll off your back. It doesn't matter what people say. You know your clothes are clean. I think your bangs look nice," he said.

That startled her into raising her head a little. She wiped her cheek with the back of her hand. "Excuse me?"

"Your bangs." He gestured toward them with one hand, nearly touching them, but not. "I think they look nice, even if you cut them yourself. Don't let the gossip get to you."

"I—I—" She had no idea where this new information fit in. "I don't understand." But she did. People in the hospital must have been making fun of her homemade haircut. Jamie had heard them.

Her humiliation was absolute. Everyone saw through her charade of respectability. Everyone scorned her attempts to act like she had a normal life and a normal job at this hospital. Everyone except Jamie.

Instead of scorning her, Jamie pitied her. For a month, she'd eaten lunch with him and let herself believe he was her friend, but the truth was, he pitied her. A man didn't ask a woman to be his celibate wife if he didn't think she was rock-bottom hopeless.

Kendry sat all the way up, and this time he let her. Then he sat up, too, straightened his tie, and dusted her cracker crumbs off his lap. The cellophane wrapper she was still holding must not have been empty, after all.

Embarrassed, she tucked that fist into her own lap. "Sorry."

"No big deal. Sam makes a much bigger mess than you do."

"A big mess," she repeated. She forced a little laugh. "That about sums it up. I'm a big mess."

"I didn't say that."

Oh, but he had. It was the truth, and it hurt to hear. She'd made a mess of her life, and she knew it.

"Your hair looks nice. Your clothes are clean. You are never late to work, and you are exceptional at your job. You're not a mess, Kendry, and I don't want to hear you think that way about yourself."

Kendry didn't want to think about anything at all. She was exhausted. She bent to grab the plastic bag at her feet that held her dirty scrubs, the ones she had to go home and clean in a tiny bathroom sink that she shared with three other people, the sink she had to clean first, before she could clean her scrubs in it. She threw her trash in the bag.

"My life is a mess, Jamie. It's the truth. Sorry if it offends you."

"It's not that you offended me," he began, but then he stopped and practically glared at her. "Check that. Yes, you did offend me. I asked you to marry me. Do you think I'd ask a 'big mess' to be the mother of my child?"

There was no other kind of person he could have expected to say yes. Pain made her lash out.

"You want to secure some kind of permanent nanny for Sam. Your proposal wasn't what Prince Charming said to Cinderella, was it? 'Come to my castle and take care of my kid.'"

"I'm offering you much more than that. We'll be a family."

"You have a family. You need a babysitter. If you'd asked me to be your babysitter, I might have said yes. It depends if you pay better than the hospital."

Jamie stood abruptly. "It's not about money, and it isn't about babysitters, but if that's what it boils down to for you—"

She looked up at him, dry-eyed, angry. "That's exactly what it boiled down to, Jamie. You offered me marriage to get yourself a free babysitter. You thought I was so pitiful I'd take you up on it. Well, the answer is no."

"No? You're turning me down?"

She couldn't believe he still thought she'd say yes. Was she that pitiful, then?

Look at yourself. Crying over fifty-dollar scrubs. Eating free crackers. He must have thought you were a sure thing.

Pride kept her chin high and her voice even. "I'm not as desperate as you think, Dr. MacDowell. Of course I said no."

He left. Without another word, he walked toward the hospital with his usual stride. Purposeful, swift. Not a backward glance. Not a goodbye.

As she watched him walk away, her heart hurt even more than her empty stomach. Jamie wasn't heading for the E.R. He was going toward the tower that held the playroom. Kendry understood perfectly. She wished she could hold sweet Sam, rest her cheek on his perfectly soft hair and feel loved.

Instead, she had to go wait for the city bus.

With filthy scrubs in a trash bag.

With the horrible knowledge that she'd picked a fight with a man who didn't deserve it.

Chapter Nine

Jamie wanted his motorcycle back.

It was completely and utterly impractical for a father. Sam couldn't be transported on it, so Jamie had sold the bike to Quinn. He regretted that sale when he needed to clear his mind.

Kendry didn't want to be married to him. Kendry didn't want to be Sam's mother.

Twice in his life, Jamie had asked a woman to marry him. Twice, he'd been told no. At least Amina had chosen to stay in Afghanistan, where marriage to him was legally impossible, because she'd wanted to help her countrymen. But Kendry—

Jamie pushed the door open to the physicians' lounge in the E.R. with too much force, making it bang against the wall.

Kendry hadn't given him any reason at all. She'd sat on a bench and bawled over a set of new scrubs, and he'd felt sorry for her. *Sorry* for her, as if getting her feelings hurt fell anywhere on the same scale as saving children in a third-world nation.

Jamie rifled through the lab coat he'd left in the locker, looking for his truck keys. Quinn would use his truck while he used the bike, no questions asked. If Jamie had any hope of restoring a sense of calm, he needed to feel some speed and some wind and let his asinine, ridiculous feelings about Kendry get blown away by the highway.

That little scrap of a girl had insulted him. Kendry thought he was a simpleton for suggesting that her supervisor could have called the E.R. for fresh scrubs. *You have no idea what it's like to be at the bottom of the totem pole.*

Fine.

She didn't think his proposal was good enough. *Come to my castle and take care of my kid.*

Fine.

Jamie dug the motorcycle's key out of Quinn's gym bag, put his truck keys in its place and slammed the locker shut.

He'd said her hair looked nice, damn it. Wasn't that what women wanted to hear? Hell, he deserved an Oscar for his performance, trying to make her feel like she wasn't a big mess.

She *was* a big mess. She refused to do anything about her allergies, she was forever eating crackers and trailing crumbs, and she didn't care about getting new glasses.

Still, she'd turned down his marriage proposal. Life with a successful, decent man like himself hadn't been good enough for sloppy, messy Kendry Harrison.

He started to walk through the kitchenette, his gaze going to the coffeepot where the three nurses had smugly laughed at Kendry after calling her...

He stopped.

Calling her exactly what he'd just thought. He hadn't said "homely" or "street urchin" like they had, not exactly, but he was focusing on the surface things, on her physical appearance, when he'd asked her to marry him for deeper reasons.

He stared absently at the coffeepot, then at the wall behind it, automatically reading the piece of paper taped to the wall, the flyer that food services put out every week.

This Week's Specials:
Enchilada Casserole
Vegetarian Lasagna
Free refills on soup, Monday through Friday

Pieces started falling into place. Bits of information, coalescing into a new theory. The taped glasses, the refusal to buy over-the-counter allergy medicine—it all came together.
Free refills on soup, Monday through Friday.

He was an idiot. Blind. How many times had he teased Kendry for loving soup? Free refills—it was all she ate, all he ever saw her eat. God, she probably ate soup all day long.

Except today. She'd had no soup bowl on the picnic bench. Crackers, always the free crackers, but nothing else. Not when they were docking her pay for the cost of her scrubs.

He'd chalked up her tears to chafing under a supervisor's orders, but she'd been worried about the cost. He'd sat next to her on a picnic bench and lectured her about being too sensitive while she'd exchanged her lunch for scrubs she hadn't wanted.

Kendry wasn't some college kid, living on student loans. Kendry lived in poverty.

It was like a punch in the gut. He thought highly of Kendry, very highly. She had every quality that would be important if she became Sam's mother. He enjoyed being around her. He thought of her as a friend.

And he, he who had grown up on a prosperous ranch, he who'd banked the military bonuses for being a doctor and for being in a combat zone, adding those extra thousands to

the accounts he'd already inherited from his father, *he* had
spent a month watching his friend, too thin as she was, eat
bowl after bowl of free soup refills.

Jamie headed outside toward the park bench. Kendry
wasn't there, and he'd already learned from the playroom
staff that she was done for the day. He started running toward the parking lot, aware that he was turning heads. It
didn't matter. He needed to find Kendry and make things
right. Now. Her shift was over, so she'd be going home, and
he had no idea where her home was.

Did she have a home?

He'd failed her. The woman was going to eat nothing
today, nothing except crackers. With every pound of his foot
on the pavement, the thought repeated in his mind: *I failed
her.* He'd offered her marriage, confident she would accept,
but he hadn't made sure she had a damned sandwich to eat.

Every moment it took to find the bike, to don the helmet, to fire up the engine, was another moment away from
Kendry. Jamie drove the motorcycle through the labyrinth
of hospital buildings, looking for one woman among the
pedestrians, since it was now painfully obvious to him that
Kendry couldn't afford a car.

He caught a glimpse of her—her hair, plain and brown,
her scrubs, new and pink—as she boarded the city bus at
the next corner. He shouted her name, but his voice only
bounced around inside the motorcycle helmet.

The bus was easy to follow. It was harder to dodge the
black exhaust that bellowed out every time the bus merged
back into traffic, but Jamie stayed immediately behind it,
watching to see if Kendry was one of the passengers who
stepped onto the pavement at each stop.

It was hardest of all to dodge his own thoughts. He gave
up trying. He deserved every mental lash he gave himself.
Every scrap of a memory that caused him pain, he deserved.

Just leave your tray, Dr. MacDowell. I'll take it up with

mine. He'd walked away and never looked back to see that she was undoubtedly buttering the roll he hadn't wanted, or finishing the apple pie he'd only eaten half of.

What kind of man let a woman starve in front of him? The bus belched more black smoke, and he put the motorcycle in gear to follow.

Primitive, caveman feelings he hadn't felt in ages came to the fore. He was male and she was female. He was bigger and stronger; he ought to have been protecting her.

In Afghanistan, he—and probably every soldier there, male and female alike—had felt the frustration of not being able to protect the helpless, the children, the women who still hid in their burqas, afraid to trust that the Taliban would not return to power. They'd all done what they could, both as soldiers and as individuals.

There had been native Afghanis willing to fight for the helpless, as well. People like Amina. Near the end, as her pregnancy became obvious and the local situation deteriorated, he and Amina had fought, every day, about her desire to keep crusading and his desire to bring her to the States, to London, to anywhere safe. They'd never reconciled their goals as an unmarried, doomed couple.

In the end, none of it had mattered. Jamie hadn't been able to save Amina from the same thing that killed an appalling number of women in Afghanistan: childbirth.

He'd failed to convince Amina to stay with him.

He'd failed to convince Kendry.

He faltered, letting go of the motorcycle's throttle. The bus moved on without him.

He couldn't go through this again. He couldn't chase a woman and beg her to let him protect her, plead with her to stay where he could keep her safe.

He couldn't, he wouldn't, endure the heartache when the woman refused his offer of help.

Don't lose it, Jamie. This is Kendry you're thinking of,

not Amina. Kendry isn't going to die if she refuses to live with you.

No, but she'd go hungry. Jamie would be damned before he'd let Kendry go hungry any longer.

The feelings were new, yet familiar at the same time. He'd felt this way about Amina when she'd told him she was pregnant, an absolute surety that he accepted the responsibility for one woman. He couldn't feel this protective of Kendry, too.

Sam's second mother? You don't think you should feel protective of her?

Put that way, it made perfect sense that he needed to take care of Kendry. If they married, he'd be the provider, after all. He felt protective of Sam, so he was feeling protective of Sam's new mother.

Jamie turned the throttle, caught up to the bus. This possessive feeling was completely different than his feelings for Amina.

His cell phone vibrated in his pocket again, as it had at least a half dozen times during this low-speed, pollution-filled pursuit. He wouldn't answer it while he was in traffic. He'd sewn up the aftermath of too many drivers checking their cell phones while on the road.

At last, in an obviously low-income neighborhood, Kendry stepped off the bus.

She looked as pitiful as the hospital grapevine said. The new pink scrubs hung too loosely on her frame. Her eyes were downcast, her ponytail drooped, and it looked like raising one hand to shield her eyes from the Texas sun took all her energy. Jamie felt a twisting emotion, deep inside.

He pulled over to the curb and silenced his bike. She'd turned on the sidewalk and was headed toward him, so he took off his helmet and waited until she came closer. She didn't see him, shading her eyes the way she was. It sickened him to realize she couldn't afford sunglasses.

"Kendry."

"Dr. MacDowell! What are you doing here?"

For a second, his mind went blank. He was here because she was here—but that wasn't what he was supposed to say. He'd come to tell her one hundred things. He started with the most important one. "I'm sorry. I'm so sorry, Kendry. You were right. My proposal came out all wrong."

She walked closer to him, so he stayed seated on the bike, keeping their faces on the same level.

"You didn't have to follow me home for that," she said. "I knew you'd change your mind. You'd have to be crazy to really want to marry me for any reason." She held her bag of old scrubs away from her body.

"I haven't changed my mind about anything." Homeless people leaned against the wall of the gas station behind her, making an apathetic audience. "Sam hasn't changed his mind about you, either. I still want you to marry me."

She made something of a little squeaky sound at that, and looked away. The incessant vibrating of his cell phone was getting to him, so he impatiently took it out of his leather jacket's pocket, glancing at the screen as he silenced it.

Sam.

Jamie had left him safely at the hospital's playroom, of course. He wasn't due to pick him up for hours yet, because he'd been scheduled for an after-lunch staff meeting—a meeting he'd blown off to follow a city bus. The message on the phone's screen made his heart stop for a second. Finances and soup and scrubs were wiped from his brain.

"What's wrong?" Kendry asked.

"Sam," he managed to say. "He's in the E.R."

"Oh, God."

"Let's go." He gestured toward the back of the bike, and Kendry only hesitated for a second before she got on. It was all so obvious. He needed to be with Sam, and he needed

Kendry to be there, too, by his side—or rather, his son needed Kendry to be by *his* side.

He handed her the helmet. "Put that on." He stood to kick-start the bike.

Over the roar of the engine, Kendry hollered, "You wear it."

He shook his head impatiently. It wasn't against the law to ride a bike without a helmet in Texas; it was just a foolish risk. Desperate times called for desperate measures. As imperative as it had been to get to Kendry, it was now to get back to Sam—but he was taking Kendry with him, no question. He'd not leave her to starve for the rest of the day.

"Put the helmet on, damn it."

When she tried to balance her plastic bag on her thigh in order to take the heavy helmet, he picked the bag up and hurled it toward the gas station's open trash can. "I'm getting you new scrubs."

He was a jackass for giving her orders. He shrugged out of the leather jacket, then twisted toward her, holding it open so she could put her arms in it. "Please. Put this on, please." She was fragile. He didn't want her hurt. Period.

"Be extra careful," she said, as she tentatively set her hands at his hips.

"Hold on tighter. Like this." He pulled her hands all the way around his stomach, then let go and pulled away from the curb, hands on the handlebars.

Hang in there, Sam. I'm on my way. Kendry and I are on our way.

Chapter Ten

Kendry clung to Jamie hard and prayed even harder. They were parking under the eaves by the E.R.'s sliding glass door in half the time it took the city bus to get there. It was startling how close she lived to the hospital, really. Commuting by bus took so much time, Kendry had always felt so far away.

Jamie had not sped nor broken a single traffic law the entire way back, but Kendry had felt his tension in her body, pressed as she'd been against his back. There was nothing she could do to comfort him, nothing she could say to reassure a man whose child was in his own E.R. Maybe she'd kept her arms wrapped around him a little too tightly, wanting things to turn out okay for him. Maybe he'd assumed she'd been scared to fall off the motorcycle.

The security guard leaped up to stop him as Jamie headed through the sliding glass doors like he owned them. With a curt nod at the guard, Jamie kept walking. Kendry wasn't swift enough, so the guard held out his hand and stopped her before she could enter the building. "Who's he?"

"That's Dr. MacDowell," Kendry answered, looking through the glass door, watching Jamie's back recede as he strode swiftly down the linoleum aisle toward the nurses' station. Toward Sam. She felt ill with worry.

"And who are you?"

Kendry hesitated, unsure what to say. Confessing she was an off-duty orderly who was unrelated to any patient in the E.R. wasn't going to get her anywhere.

The security guard crossed his arms over his chest in something of an aggressive stance. "You can't leave that bike here."

Kendry still wore Jamie's leather jacket. It swallowed her whole rather than lend her any biker swagger, but she decided to act like Jamie, anyway. She nodded once at the guard like Jamie had. "I'll tell him to move it," she said, and walked toward the doors like a woman with a purpose.

It worked. The guard didn't reach out to stop her, the doors whooshed open, and Kendry walked purposefully down the aisle, shrugging out of the leather coat as she went. She got close enough to Jamie to almost make out what the nurse was saying to him, picking out words like *cyanotic* and *oxygen*.

"Which bed?" Jamie demanded impatiently.

Kendry wanted to shake the nurse. *He's not this baby's doctor; he's his father. He wants to hold his son, not hear a medical report.*

Jamie headed for bed three. So did Kendry, but another hand reached out to stop her. "There you are," the nurse said. "We're low on linens."

"I'm sorry, but I'm off the clock." Kendry watched Jamie disappear into one of the private cubicles that had a door. Bed three.

The nurse was looking at Kendry's scrubs and frowning. "Where's your ID?"

"I'm off the clock," she repeated. "I'm sorry, but I've got to go see a patient."

"Who?" the nurse asked, as though it were a fantastical improbability that Kendry might know a single patient personally.

It burned. Kendry had never felt so impatient in her life. Sam was here, sweet little Sam, and she had no idea how he was doing. Jamie wanted her to be with him—with Sam, that is. The guard and now the nurse were stopping her.

"Sam MacDowell," she said through gritted teeth. "He was brought down from the peds ward."

The nurse frowned harder. "His father just got here. It's family only back here. You know that."

"But…it's Sam. I want to see him."

"If you're not here to work, you can leave through the waiting room. HIPAA regulations are very clear about—"

"Kendry." The voice that spoke her name was quiet, authoritative, male.

She and the nurse turned toward Jamie. He was standing just outside the door of bed three, his hand held out to her. Feeling like the out-of-place orderly she was, Kendry thought he wanted his jacket back. She put it in his outstretched hand.

Jamie frowned at her, like the guard and the nurse, but he took the jacket and very deliberately held out his other hand. Kendry ignored the heat in her cheeks as she put her hand in his. His fingers closed around hers, warm and firm, and he tugged her with him into the room.

Sammy, so tiny, lay in the middle of an adult-sized treatment bed. The side rails had been raised, and some additional padded buffers had been placed around him to keep him from rolling off.

Sammy didn't look like he was in any condition to roll

anywhere. One of his arms was being held straight by a green plastic splint, a tiny needle and thin IV tube coming out of the crease at his elbow. A pediatric-sized oxygen mask still looked too big on his little face, covering his nose and mouth—and his whole chin, too.

"Oh, Sammy," Kendry cooed, tears blurring her vision as she dropped Jamie's hand and bent over the bed, clutching the rail's cold metal in both hands. "How's my favorite guy?"

Sammy turned toward the sound of her voice immediately. After one blink, his mouth opened wide in a big, mostly toothless smile behind the clear oxygen mask. Kendry thought her heart would burst at his cheerful attitude in his dismal situation. She couldn't help it; she had to touch him.

"I'm so glad to see you, too," she said, trying to keep her voice even as she placed her hand on his belly. Sam wriggled a little and lifted his splinted arm a fraction, but the effort apparently reminded him that he was somewhat pinned down, and he frowned.

Just like his father. As clear as day, Kendry saw Jamie's facial expression on little Sammy's face. Her favorite little guy looked just like her big dream guy. Emotions filled her, too many to name.

Jamie cleared his throat. "I think he wants you to pick him up."

As she'd done a hundred times for other patients, Kendry dropped the side railing to the bed. As she had never done before, she picked up the patient, kissed him on his soft hair and closed her eyes in gratitude that she could hug him close. "You scared us, Sammy." She kept her eyes closed for a moment longer, then stole another kiss. Sam settled into her heavily, and she could tell he'd be asleep in moments. She sat on the bed with him in her arms.

Not looking up from Sam, she asked Jamie, "Why is he here?"

"Respiratory distress."

"But he's breathing okay now?"

"Time will tell. Someone left him on his back in his crib with a bottle."

Appalled, she looked up at Jamie. "That's against policy for all the infants, let alone one with Sammy's swallowing problems."

"I know." The mattress gave a little as Jamie sat down next to her, their thighs touching as he patted Sam's back. After the motorcycle ride, she found it wasn't so unnerving to be near him physically. It was even comforting. Sheltering. It made her feel better when the sight of Sammy in his medical gear had her shaken up.

Jamie gently took the oxygen mask off Sam. "He probably choked on the formula. He may have inhaled a bit of it into his lungs. Between the choking and the coughing, he was screaming, of course. Given his heart defect, he started to turn blue from lack of oxygen."

"Oh, Sammy." Kendry rested her cheek on the top his head. She didn't want to put him down ever again. "What happens next?"

"We wait and see if he develops pneumonia from the formula getting in his lungs—if it got in his lungs. His coughing and gagging may have kept it out, like reflexes are supposed to. The respiratory distress could have been from the heart defect, not from liquid in the lungs. We'll find out this week. The hard way."

"Poor baby," Kendry whispered. "If only I had been on duty."

Jamie raised his eyebrows a little at that. "If only I *hadn't* been on duty." He surprised Kendry by standing suddenly, looking like he wanted to pace. The treatment room was too small for a man his size to take more than a half step. "Don't start feeling guilty about anything, Kendry. It will eat you up. God knows I've already screwed up enough things for ten parents to feel guilty about."

"You didn't screw up anything." She kept her voice low as Sam fell asleep. "It's not your fault someone gave Sam a bottle while he was lying flat on his back."

Jamie nearly laughed. "Yeah."

"This isn't your fault." Kendry studied him, worried. He looked a little wild, a little bit like a man on the brink, not like the controlled doctor she knew.

"I should have caught that cleft palate the day he was born."

"Don't be ridiculous. I'm sure—" She stopped, catching herself as she was about to blunder into what was probably painful territory.

"You're sure of what?"

"I'm sure that had to have been the least of your worries the day he was born." Kendry bit her lip and watched him anxiously, but Jamie didn't seem fazed by her statement. She'd only learned two nights ago that Sam's mother had died during his birth, but Jamie had been living with that horrible knowledge for nine months.

"Sam shouldn't have been born in that situation to start with. I got *him* out of Afghanistan, at least, and I've been pretending I know what I'm doing, but hell, Kendry...I don't know anything. I've failed him in a million ways. I didn't know how to hold him to feed him, for God's sake."

"But you learned. That's the important—"

"I haven't been able to get his Social Security number yet. I know he needs these surgeries, but I keep putting them off, because I don't know how to handle his recovery and my job at the same time. Hell, my family thinks I'm crazy not to hire someone else to take care of him. Maybe they are seeing the obvious. Maybe they can see that I can't take care of a baby."

"You can so. You're a wonderful parent."

"I can't give him all he needs. He needs so much. He needs a mother, too, not just me, but I—" He gestured toward her. "I can't even make a friend without screwing everything up for her. I've made you the object of gossip. I threw away your clothes an hour ago."

The scrubs were going to be a problem, but she wasn't about to lay her burdens on this man. "I'll deal with it, Jamie."

"I don't want you to. Can't you see that?"

He loomed over her, intense and serious. She kept Sammy in her arms between them.

"I don't want you to handle it," he said. "I want to take care of it for you. I want to take care of Sam, to provide for both of you, to do something right for once. I'm so tired of things going wrong. The war, Amina getting pregnant when she shouldn't have, dying when she shouldn't have, Sammy needing emergency care when he shouldn't, you needing a damned meal when you shouldn't. If I was half the man I should be, none of that would happen."

"Oh, Jamie." Kendry hadn't realized his pain, the depth of his feeling of letting everyone down. The past year of his life had to have been harrowing. Like everyone on earth, he needed a break. He needed something to go right.

"You have a wonderful little boy here," she began.

"Yes, I do," Jamie said, and the old Jamie was back. At least, the determined and confident man was back, the one who saved strangers' lives in the E.R. Only now his cool and clear focus wasn't on a patient. It was on her.

"My son is a wonderful boy. He's fallen in love with you, because you are a wonderful woman. Whether you marry me or not, Kendry Harrison, you are not going to go hungry again, and you aren't going to struggle for material things, because you deserve better than that. Sam thinks so, and so do I. But I'd rather marry you. I want to do something right. I want to be normal, and have a family, and have the legal and moral right to care for you and Sam, to build something real."

He moved toward her, as if he wanted to pull them both into his arms, but stopped short and instead stood over them, arms open, empty.

"But you're not in love with me." Kendry whispered the words as she met his clear gaze, wishing with all her heart she weren't stating a simple truth.

Very slowly, very slightly, Jamie shook his head. "My heart was buried with the woman I gave it to."

He reached out to lift her face with a touch of his warm fingers under her chin. "But that doesn't mean I'm not offering you something good. Something real. I'm offering you all I have left in me to give, and that includes my son."

Jamie dropped his hand to lightly touch Sam's hair. "I'm not offering you an easy child to love. I'm offering you one with a lot of health problems. A future of surgeries and therapies and rehab. The more you love Sam, the more it will break your heart when he's in pain. But I—I think he's worth it. I can't imagine living without him."

Her heart stopped when Jamie stopped touching Sam's hair and instead cupped her cheek. "And lately, I keep imagining a life with you. Kendry Harrison, I want to marry you."

He hadn't really asked a question, but she answered him anyway.

"Yes."

He didn't love her. He'd never love her.

But she loved him.

Chapter Eleven

"Yes."

Kendry had said yes. The rush of adrenaline had been instant. Unexpected.

It was all Jamie could do to play it cool and wait by the motorcycle for Quinn to show up with his truck, when he wanted to grab Kendry by the hand and run to the courthouse before she could change her mind.

Quinn pulled up in Jamie's practical extended-cab truck and parked it under the eaves. He had the engine off and was rounding the hood when he spotted Kendry holding Sam and stopped short. Jamie stayed where he was, leaning on the motorcycle, arms crossed over his chest. As he watched Quinn take in the scene, he started to grin.

"I believe you've already met my wife to be, Kendry."

Quinn lifted a brow in question, looking so much like their father that Jamie felt a brief pang.

"Well." That was it. That was all Quinn could come up with.

Jamie would have enjoyed the moment of Quinn's speechlessness longer, but Kendry was looking acutely embarrassed. "It's not like we're—"

Jamie put his hand on Kendry's shoulder—God, she was all bones—and dropped the bike keys in Quinn's hand. "We've got to run. Thanks for bringing the truck back so quickly."

"I had no desire to continue to drive around town in a truck with a baby's car seat in the backseat. It could've killed my reputation with the ladies."

"Or it could've made it. Babies are chick magnets. Sam caught me a wife, see?" Jamie nodded toward Kendry, willing her to not look scared to death of his brother.

Before Jamie could think of the right thing to say to put her at ease, Quinn snapped out of his shock and proceeded to give Kendry a bear hug, despite Sam in her arms, and a kiss on the cheek for good measure.

"Welcome to the family, then, sis."

Good old Quinn, the mathematical cardiologist. Like their father had always done, Quinn neatly categorized everything he encountered. If Kendry was Jamie's wife, then that made her family. Family got a hug and a welcome. Plain and simple.

Dad would have acted like Quinn.

Somehow, the idea that his father would have accepted Kendry as his daughter-in-law made the knot in Jamie's gut feel just a little—just slightly—looser. Which made no sense at all, because Jamie was trying to be a different kind of father than the one who'd raised him. Or rather, different than the one who hadn't been there much at all to raise him.

Impatiently, Jamie snapped Sam into his car seat in the back bench of the pickup truck. Whether his father would have approved or not was irrelevant. If his father had taught him anything, it was that if a boy didn't have a mother, he'd be a lonely child, indeed.

It was time to get Kendry Harrison to the courthouse.

Kendry sat in the backseat of the truck's cab so she could keep an eye on Sam. Her little guy was sleeping hard, exhausted from his afternoon of choking and coughing, but he was otherwise fine. Kendry couldn't help looking at him every two minutes to reaffirm that fact.

Jamie didn't need her beside him, anyway. During the few minutes they'd waited for Quinn to arrive with the truck, Jamie had used his phone to learn everything he needed to know about getting married in Austin.

They'd breezed through a fast-food drive-through on the way to their first stop, since Jamie insisted she needed a burger and a shake. Kendry felt a little guilty for not putting up much of a fight on that point. Then they'd driven on to the Travis County Clerk of Courts, which wasn't in the main courthouse, but rather in a one-story plaza in an unremarkable part of town. Unremarkable, if she didn't count the building on the opposite side of the street, a warehouse whose sign was a two-story-tall candy cane with a lamb dangling from it. The candy cane looked to be leaning away from the old candy factory it marked, cantilevered at a crazy angle with its motorcycle-sized lamb dangling by a thread…

It was all so bizarre. This whole day was bizarre. Kendry slurped the last drop of the shake as quietly as she could. She looked at Sam. He was sleeping peacefully, but it was quite possible that his lungs were battling an infection while she sipped a strawberry shake.

The clerk's offices weren't empty, but it seemed all the people they ran into were on their way out of the building. Perhaps the good citizens of Austin were in a rush to get back to their jobs after running an errand on their lunch hour. Whatever the reason, she and Jamie and Sammy were the only ones eager to go into the government building, rather than out of it.

Eager? Was she eager to reach the marriage license window?

This was not, ever, the way she'd imagined getting married. Not in a rush. Not wearing scrubs that still felt stiff and itchy in their newness. Not lugging a sleeping baby in his car seat, and not with a man who wasn't in love with her.

But he did love her, in some small way. Or rather, he loved the idea of making her Sam's mother. He loved the idea of being a settled, married man. He was grateful to her.

And she, Kendry Harrison, was settling for less than she really wanted. Again. An orderly instead of a nurse. A mother instead of a lover. She should stop this marriage.

"The marriage license is seventy-one dollars. We only take cash."

The clerk was more concerned with the cash than she was with verifying that the two people standing in front of her were eligible to be married. A casual look at their driver's licenses was all it took for the paperwork to cross the counter.

"You have to wait three days before you can get married," the clerk explained.

Kendry saw Jamie's pen stop in midstroke on the paperwork.

"Three days?" he asked.

"There's a seventy-two-hour waiting period."

Three days. This crazy idea that today, a random Thursday in September, would be her wedding day, ended. They had time to come to their senses. Jamie surely would change his mind, and she would not be his wife.

She looked at the set of his jaw, at his close-cropped hair, military in its style, at the way he kept one hand on Sam's car seat, always keeping that baby safe, although the seat was securely sitting on a wide desk.

Suddenly, she didn't want to wait. Jamie would change

his mind, and she would lose him. And lose Sam. And lose the feeling of being wanted and needed.

She was worried about compromising, about settling for being Jamie's platonic wife. But when faced with not being his wife at all, she realized this was one compromise she was willing to make. She wanted, more than anything, to get married on this Thursday to this man, while wearing brand-new pink scrubs and holding her brand-new sleeping son.

"Three days will be Sunday," Jamie said.

"Yep," the clerk said, after dutifully checking her desk calendar.

"I'm in the army. I have to report to my new unit tomorrow night. Friday."

"Oh," the clerk said, brightening. "If you're active-duty military, you don't have to wait. Just show your military ID to the justice of the peace. The closest one who might do a wedding today is at the courthouse on Guadalupe Street."

Jamie looked as relieved as Kendry felt. Briskly, he held the door open for her, then drew her to his side as they headed for the truck. "Let's go right now. Today."

He really wants to marry me.

Kendry smiled at him.

He didn't smile back but gave her the smallest of squeezes before letting go. "I have to turn in my active-duty ID when I report to my reserve unit tomorrow night. We made it in the nick of time."

Or maybe he was just an efficient kind of groom.

Efficient was an understatement. Her actual wedding had been a blur, a handing over of paperwork and IDs, a local judge who was willing to spend his break between scheduled hearings to earn an extra hundred dollars, and a civil exchange of vows. The judge skipped the part about exchanging rings and pronounced them man and wife. Jamie had quickly thanked him before the judge could say anything like, "You may now kiss the bride," so that part was eliminated as easily as the rings. Minutes later, Jamie was checking his watch as he opened the passenger door for Kendry.

"I think Sam's going to sleep a little longer," he said. "Let's go replace those scrubs I threw away."

Kendry began her married life at a big-box store, pushing a shopping cart and keeping an eye on Sam. He slept in the car seat, which snapped into place on the cart's handle. On their way to the back of the store, Jamie passed a display for the melt-in-the-mouth kind of allergy medicine. "This one works fast," he said, "so take it now, and you'll be feeling better by the time we leave."

She meekly obeyed the doctor's orders, especially after the man opened the package and put the pill in her hand. They had to pay for the opened package, so there was no sense arguing. She could practically see Jamie checking an item off his imaginary mental list: *Treat allergies. Check.*

In the uniform department, Kendry carefully selected one set of scrubs in her size. Jamie grabbed four more sets and tossed them in the cart. He made a beeline for the shoe department. "I don't think Sam's going to sleep long enough for me to get you something nicer, but these will be better than nothing for work tomorrow."

Kendry looked down at her sneakers. Compared to the new pink scrubs, they looked horribly worn. She wanted to point out that these would last another day, but Jamie was already halfway down the aisle of women's shoes. It took her longer to try on sneakers than it had to say "I do," although she only tried on two pair. When she said, "These fit fine," Jamie produced a pocketknife, cut the tags off the new ones and threw her old pair into the box and then the cart.

It was embarrassing to see his hands handling her battered sneakers. She gave up pretending this was a normal shopping trip on a normal day, and silently followed Jamie through the store, mustering a smile and a nod when he asked her if she needed socks, too.

Get the orderly outfitted for work tomorrow. Check.

Jamie was practically in full E.R. doctor mode, a man on a mission, and he didn't need her input. He led the way to the baby aisle. Kendry kept calculating how much it would all cost. The diapers and formula alone were enough to pay her rent. Jamie didn't seem to care. In fact, he kept adding more baby items to the cart, more concerned with which brand of teething biscuits Sam would enjoy than with which brand cost the least.

Kendry hadn't set foot in a major supermarket in a year. It was too time-consuming and expensive to switch buses to get from the inner city out to the suburbs, so she bought things like cereal in overpriced gas stations. She'd forgotten how colorful the superstores were, how high the ceilings, how many different brands of everything filled shelf after shelf. It was dazzling. It made her want to cry.

Sam began to cry instead. Kendry unbuckled him from the seat and held him close, grateful for the comfort she received from comforting him. *He* was important. *He* was what it was all about.

"Here, let me hold Sam while you get what you need." Jamie lifted Sam off her hip with a "hey, buddy," and waited patiently by the cart.

Kendry looked around, then felt herself blush. She'd followed Jamie into the cosmetics aisle.

"I don't wear makeup." She tried not to squirm when Jamie automatically looked at her face—not at her, but at the surface of her. Her skin and stuff. She couldn't stand it; she put her hands on her blushing cheeks. "I probably should, I know, but—"

"Why should you?"

She dropped her hands. "I don't know. It gives women a more professional appearance, I guess." As soon as she said that, she thought of her hasty, homemade haircut and tugged on her bangs.

Jamie spoke to Sam. "Do you think Kendry needs to look more professional?"

Sam cooed and stuck his fingers in his mouth.

"Me, neither," he said, smiling at Sam before turning back to Kendry. "We like you just the way you are. If you want makeup, go for it. If you don't, that's fine, too." He nodded at the shelves behind her. "You at least need some shampoo and items like that."

"Oh! Shampoo!" She whirled to the shelf behind her. She'd been using one bar of soap for her face, body and hair for so long now, she'd forgotten the luxury of having separate products. Soap was soap, and they all did the same job, but Jamie would think she was weird if she didn't use shampoo, wouldn't he? She didn't want him to think she was weird.

That was her excuse to start touching the bottles. She even picked up a couple, popping their caps open for a quick sniff of heavenly fruits and flowers. Thanks to that tiny allergy pill, her nose was actually drying up enough to smell something. The ginger and lemongrass shampoo smelled so good, she held it up for Sam to smell, too. Then she put it back on the shelf and bent down to pick up the economy-sized bottle of the store-brand shampoo.

"Okay," she said, placing the bottle in the cart. "Next aisle."

"Kendry." Jamie sounded hoarse. He looked angry.

Her hand hovered over the bottle. "I'm sorry, is it too much? I wasn't thinking—I mean, it probably looks greedy, doesn't it? But it's cheaper per ounce and it won't expire—"

"Kendry." But Jamie didn't say anything else. Instead, with Sam in one arm, he grabbed the ginger-lemongrass shampoo off the shelf and placed it in the cart. Then he grabbed the matching conditioner, too.

She was going to cry. It was humiliating, being so poor,

making do, pretending you didn't want all the products you couldn't afford. Sam started fussing and reaching for her, wriggling to get down from his father's arms. Children had a way of picking up the tension around them.

Jamie handed Sam to her. "Money's been tight for you, I can tell, but we're a family now. Sam deserves the best I can give him, and Sam's mother deserves the same. Please, pick out whatever you need."

He touched her under the chin, a move she was certain he meant to be comforting. Maybe, like Sam, Jamie could sense that she was on edge. For the first time in hours, he smiled at her. "We'll still be able to send Sam to college, I promise."

She smiled back, because she wanted to pretend everything was okay, that she wasn't the most pitiful bride ever, and this wasn't the least romantic wedding day in history. Then she threw into the cart a facial cleanser and a lotion that had sunscreen in it.

Just as they were leaving the aisle, she grabbed a lip gloss and tossed it in with the rest, telling herself it had nothing to do with the warmth of the man's fingers as he'd lifted her chin.

Chapter Twelve

The trip to the superstore landed Kendry in an optometrist's office. She'd paused at the rack of reading glasses that looked like the ones Sammy had broken. Jamie's interrogation had begun, and he'd insisted she get a proper prescription. She'd agreed to make an appointment. Soon.

Jamie's idea of soon was to call a friend, an optometrist who immediately made room in her schedule for them. Kendry suspected the optometrist, who was very pretty and very blonde, wasn't terribly thrilled to find out she was helping a female friend of Jamie's and not Jamie himself.

If she finds out Jamie is no longer a bachelor, she's really going to be unhappy.

She didn't find out. When they were alone in the exam room and the optometrist needed Kendry's last name for the vision prescription, Kendry said "Harrison" without thinking, and that was that.

Next patient.

When the staff member who was supposed to help

For Your Reading Pleasure...

Get 2 FREE BOOKS where contemporary heroines find the balance between their work life and personal life on the way to true love.

Free

Your **2 FREE BOOKS** have a combined cover price of $11.00 in the U.S. and $12.50 in Canada.

Peel off sticker and place by your completed Poll on the right page and you'll automatically receive **2 FREE BOOKS** and **2 FREE GIFTS** with no obligation to purchase anything!

YOUR OPINION POLL
THANK-YOU FREE GIFTS INCLUDE:

▶ **2 HARLEQUIN® SPECIAL EDITION BOOKS**

▶ **2 LOVELY SURPRISE GIFTS**

OFFICIAL OPINION POLL

YOUR OPINION COUNTS!
Please check TRUE or FALSE below to express your opinion about the following statements:

Q1 Do you believe in "true love"?

"TRUE LOVE HAPPENS ONLY ONCE IN A LIFETIME."
○ TRUE
○ FALSE

Q2 Do you think marriage has any value in today's world?

"YOU CAN BE TOTALLY COMMITTED TO SOMEONE WITHOUT BEING MARRIED."
○ TRUE
○ FALSE

Q3 What kind of books do you enjoy?

"A GREAT NOVEL MUST HAVE A HAPPY ENDING."
○ TRUE
○ FALSE

YES! I have placed my sticker in the space provided below. Please send me the **2 FREE books** and **2 FREE gifts** for which I qualify. I understand that I am under no obligation to purchase anything further, as explained on the back of this card.

235/335 HDL F4WD

FIRST NAME

LAST NAME

ADDRESS

APT.#

CITY

STATE/PROV.

ZIP/POSTAL CODE

Kendry select new frames for that prescription began fetching frames from displays labeled Versace and Gucci, Kendry had to protest.

"I need something for everyday. Nothing fancy. I'm with babies all day, and I'm not always fast enough to dodge them, you see?" She waved the old taped frames, which she held in her hand, hoping her explanation accounted for dime-store plastic in this shiny world of designer frames.

Thanks to the dilating eye drops Kendry had been given, the office grew brighter as her vision grew blurrier. By the time Kendry was persuaded to order the wire-thin, flexible frames that a child could bend without harming, along with invisible lenses that were supposed to be nearly impossible to break, a headache was clearly starting. The saleswoman placed the taped-up old frames in a new case and assured her they'd put in a rush order—as a professional courtesy, of course.

Kendry tried to muster a smile before returning to the waiting room. She was grateful that the office provided disposable sunglasses, a thin rectangle of plastic brown film with paper earpieces.

Jamie was talking quietly to Sam, who sat in his father's lap and waved his empty bottle in the air, turning it this way and that with serious concentration. Kendry was content to stand, unnoticed, and watch Jamie and Sam, together. It was the first time Jamie had looked relaxed since...

She racked her brain. Since the night they'd worked together in the E.R.? The night he'd sat on the bench with the rain falling beyond them, right before he'd told her they didn't have *that* kind of relationship?

Kendry watched him a moment more. Somehow, when a big man held a little baby, it made him look all the bigger and more masculine. Jamie smiled while Sammy babbled at him as if he were speaking in complete baby sentences, explaining something fully, and Kendry could see the traces of laugh lines at the corner of her new husband's eyes.

Yes, he'd been unhappy since that rainy night, but now that they'd gotten married, he looked relaxed again. Her heart did a little flip. Being married to her mattered to him.

Sammy spotted her, promptly let go of his bottle so that it clattered onto the floor, then held up both arms with his little hands open. "Me."

Jamie looked her way immediately. Like watching something bad happen in slow motion, Kendry watched a frown take over Jamie's expression. Maybe even anger.

Her heart fell. He'd never been angry with her, not until today. Their wedding day.

"You need sunglasses," he said, scooping the bottle up with one hand, hiking up Sam in his other arm. He practically stalked toward her.

"O-only for the next couple of hours," she said, alarmed. "These drops wear off fast."

"This is Texas. You need sunglasses. Good ones, to protect your eyes from UV rays." He gestured for her to go ahead of him, back toward the frames and mirrors, then pulled the chair out for her. She sat.

I'm not your patient, she wanted to say. *I'm not your employee.* But because the saleswoman was eagerly standing by, Kendry held her tongue.

Jamie removed the disposable plastic rectangle from her face and started slipping sunglasses on her himself. He was quick about it, focused, like he was choosing the right needle for a medical procedure. The pair Jamie liked best cost more than three weeks of her rent. They were still cheaper than the other sunglasses that made his cut, so Kendry agreed with his choice.

As Jamie handed his credit card to the receptionist, Sam started his fussy cry, the one that said he'd had enough and this wasn't where he wanted to be or what he wanted to be doing. Kendry bounced him on her hip as she waited by the exit. "Me, too, honey, I feel just the same," she whispered.

Jamie walked up and reached around her to push the door open. For a moment, the three of them brushed bodies as Jamie gestured for Kendry to leave first. Sam grabbed for her new sunglasses.

"No," she said, jerking her head an inch to dodge his inaccurate fist. "We can't afford to break these."

Jamie spoke quietly in her ear, words that sounded measured, but like he said them through clenched teeth. "Yes, we can."

Kendry squeezed Sam a little tighter as they walked to the car. Sam was tired. She was tired.

Jamie was angry.

This wasn't where she wanted to be or what she wanted to be doing, so she took a breath and dared to speak her mind.

"I think it's time for me to go home."

Home. The word paralyzed Jamie for a moment.

Today was the first day of making a new home for his son and himself. Could a man make a home with a woman he didn't love?

Sudden doubt filled him.

Sam protested being set in his car seat, although Jamie had parked the truck in the shade of a tree, and the Texas heat wasn't unbearable in September at this late hour of the day. Out of the corner of Jamie's eye, he could see Kendry standing with her shoulders and her ponytail drooping, waiting to get in the backseat next to Sam.

"Let's go get something to eat first, before we go home." He just needed time. Just a little longer before he brought Kendry to his house. Permanently.

Did you carry a bride over the threshold when you were going to be parents and partners, but not lovers?

"Aren't you worried about Sam?" she asked.

Jamie glanced through the open door at Sam, who had settled into his straps. "I'm always worried about Sam," he said.

Now I'm worried about my wife on top of that.

He couldn't say that out loud, not to a woman who was clearly too thin beneath her new scrubs and sneakers and sunglasses.

Kendry rubbed her forehead as she looked at Sam, too. "Maybe he needs to get home so he can sleep in his own crib. What if he's fighting off pneumonia at this very second? What if we expose him to more germs at a restaurant? What if—"

"I don't waste a lot of time on if. There's always another if waiting to happen."

Kendry looked away from him quickly.

Jamie looked in the other direction. That had sounded kind of harsh, he supposed. Kendry had no idea that the main reason Jamie had wanted to be married was to prevent a big State Department *if* from happening. She could become the key to Sam staying in Jamie's custody, if…

Jamie was glad to have Kendry on his team and by his side, yet here he was, making a mess of their first day together. He still hadn't found his balance after chasing down her bus at lunchtime. He'd practically forced her back to the E.R. with him, then to the licensing office, the courthouse, the grocery store, the optometrist. He hadn't stopped to catch his breath, which meant she hadn't had a chance to, either. "Let's go somewhere we can sit for dinner. Sam will be fine."

She looked back at him then, but he couldn't read her expression behind the sunglasses. Her shoulders rose, then fell slightly, and he imagined he'd heard her sigh as she waited patiently for him to give her further instructions. She was so good at that, at waiting patiently while nurses and doctors and patients made their demands.

He didn't want his wife's life to be that way. When they

were off duty, he wanted her to be his partner. Instead, he'd been dragging her in and out of buildings all day, telling her what to buy. Hell, he'd even chosen those sunglasses, and now he was informing her that she would eat in a sit-down restaurant...

"Unless you want drive-through?" he asked, feeling ludicrously unsure of what to say next.

"I have a headache, and I'd like to go home." Kendry said it simply, as politely as a schoolchild. Her demeanor said she held as much hope as a student might when suggesting that a teacher change his plans.

"Maybe you have a headache from hunger. There are a couple of different places to eat near my house."

Her eyebrows lifted a little, shifting the bangs that brushed the top of the dark frames. "I meant my home, not your house. I'd like to go to my home now. Unless...you aren't working the night shift tonight, are you?"

Jamie shook his head, silently. They'd only been married a few hours, and she wanted to be alone. She wanted to leave him. And Sam. She wanted to leave *them.*

She had her own life to get back to, her own agenda. It was like arguing with Amina all over again. They weren't on the same team; they didn't share the same priorities. His head swam, but he tried to listen to Kendry's next words.

"Then if you don't need me to watch Sam tonight, you can take me to my place." She said it patiently, so very patiently, like she was speaking to a child.

He was no child. He was her husband. Her husband, damn it.

"You're not the babysitter. We're married. It goes without saying, we now live together. We'll get something to eat, then we'll go to my house."

Kendry didn't move. She just stood there, wilting in the setting sun, unreadable in her sunglasses.

Jamie felt like a jerk for what seemed like the millionth

time that day. "We can stop at your place and pack up your things first, although I thought we bought enough stuff to get you through the night and to work tomorrow."

"You bought that stuff."

"What?"

"You did. You decided we would go to the store. You decided which store, and you bought that stuff. You decided to get me glasses. You decided which shampoo I would use—"

"Because you were going to buy the cheapest thing—"

"Because I don't have any money! I was being reasonable. Rational. Responsible."

"You have money now. Pardon me if I don't want my wife to wear plastic film on her face when she needs sunglasses."

"I don't have a dime. I'm not bringing anything to this marriage. Pardon me if I don't feel easy about spending someone else's money on myself. And—and—and pardon me for needing all this stuff in the first place. I'm sorry your wife embarrasses you with her taped-up glasses, but I didn't ask you to fix me. This is our first day of marriage, and I thought this was going to be all about Sam. Instead, all you've done is fix me."

Jamie was speechless. Had he just been thinking that Kendry was too patient, too willing to take orders?

She tapped her new sneaker at his silence. "You've been angry at me the whole day."

"I'm not angry at you."

"You've spent the entire afternoon with your jaw clenched, biting out your words at me. Now you've got me angry, too."

"I'm not angry at you." His words bounced off the asphalt and the metal side of the truck, vibrating in the air.

Kendry crossed her arms over her chest. "I'm glad we got that cleared up. I don't know how I could have thought you were angry."

Her sarcasm surprised him, but her next word softly and seriously, cut him to the quick.

"Honestly, Jamie, sometimes a plan sounds better ory. Actually marrying me seems to have you in knots, so let's go undo it. I don't want this."

The pain was startling. This hurt every bit as much as arguing with Amina about leaving Afghanistan. This hurt every bit as much.

He was older now. Wiser. Passionate shouting matches didn't solve anything. Hell, passion didn't solve anything. He and Kendry had always been able to talk, but now here she was—

Yes, here she was. Kendry hadn't thrown her hands in the air dramatically and stormed off to her own living quarters on a military base. She was standing right here, close enough to touch. Certainly close enough to talk to without shouting.

"You don't want this," he said, quietly affirming her words. "I do. I need this."

Kendry leaned against the truck, took off the sunglasses and rubbed her eyes. "You need to fix me?"

"Not at all. I like you the way you are. I need a partner. I need you, because you are the one I…" He hesitated, unsure how to put his feelings into words. "You're the one I trust. If I'm coming across as angry, it's because I'm mad at myself for not realizing sooner that you needed money. When I think of how much soup I watched you eat, I hate myself. I'm sorry."

She opened her eyes and looked at him. Jamie had a moment to notice how bright the green of her iris was compared to the black of her pupils.

"It's not your fault that I'm on a tight budget," she said. "In a way, it's a compliment that you didn't notice." She scrunched her eyes closed a second later with a muttered "ouch" and hastily put her sunglasses back on.

"I'm sorry for dragging you into an eye exam," Jamie

said, and he leaned against the truck next to her, feeling worn out but hopeful at the same time. She was still here.

She was still here.

"It didn't occur to me that getting new glasses meant you'd be spending your wedding day with your eyes dilated."

"It's okay," she said, and with a wave of her hand, dismissed all the inconvenience of the eye exam.

That's the way Kendry was, never carrying a chip on her shoulder, always ready to move past any obstacle. She was one of the nicest women he'd ever met.

It was why he'd married her. It was something Sam must have felt in her arms.

Jamie wanted to give her a hug. He really did.

He crossed his arms over his chest.

Kendry stole a glance at the man leaning against the truck with her, the man whose arms looked tanned and strong, muscles flexed, pulling his dress shirt taut as he crossed his arms over his chest.

"How would you have preferred to spend your wedding day?" Jamie asked.

I would have preferred to have you smiling at me in my white gown in a garden. I would have preferred to have you scoop me up with those strong arms to carry me to a white bed in a quiet room.

She hadn't agreed to that kind of marriage. She had no right to expect that kind of day.

She couldn't lie and tell him she wanted anything else, either. She was a terrible liar, so as usual, she deflected his question.

"I have a headache. I'm worried sick about Sam. I know that whether or not he gets pneumonia doesn't depend on if we take him home right this moment. I know he's sleeping just as soundly in his car seat as he would in a crib, but if I could have anything I wanted, I would go home and stretch out on a blanket on the floor next to him and fall asleep. I know being next to him won't prevent pneumonia, either, but that's what I really want to do."

"In my home?"

She heard the tentative note of hope in his serious question. She wasn't imagining it. He wanted her to say yes. He wanted her to live in his house. He wanted to be married to her. Her head hurt, but her heart lightened.

He spoke before she could answer. "Or did you want us to come to your home?" He didn't sound like a doctor anymore, no longer sounded like he was her boss. "Do you have room for us at your place? I'm not sure where you live, but if you want, Sam and I could crash at your house."

"Oh, no." She didn't want Jamie to see her place, ever. She didn't want little Sam to lie on the cement floor of the converted garage she rented by the week. "My place isn't, uh, child friendly..." Now it was her turn to trail off awkwardly.

"Jeez, we're a pitiful pair." Jamie said it with a bit of a smile on his face. He pushed away from the truck. "Let me think. What was it the prince wasn't supposed to say? 'Come to my castle and take care of my kid'?"

He rubbed the back of his neck with one hand for a moment, thinking. "Let me try this instead. Mrs. MacDowell, would you like to come to my castle and take a nap on a blanket with my kid? You can keep an eye on him, and I can cook you an omelet. I'm pretty sure the castle is low on everything except baby formula and a dozen eggs."

Kendry knew she was blushing ten shades of red. Her headache wasn't any better, but her husband's teasing eased the tension in the air. She didn't know how many times she'd already said it that day, but she said it once again: "Yes."

Chapter Thirteen

Her wedding night was sensual, in its way. She stared up at the ceiling in the darkness and felt the cold air from the vent fall on her face. The pillow was plump and deep, and smelled of fabric softener. Her stomach did not growl, and her teeth felt clean and smooth and minty. She wore her new husband's T-shirt as her nightgown. The rough cotton covered her shoulders and felt coarse on her stomach and tickled the tops of her thighs.

It wasn't the sensuality of a man, but of a man's shirt. Kendry Harrison, or rather, Kendry MacDowell, was once more settling for what she could get. She was married to a man, but she was having no wedding night. She was a guest in a bachelor's spare room, sleeping in a bed that shared space with some weight-lifting equipment and an oversize stereo.

She heard the snuffle and quiet mew of a baby. Sam. Her baby. Kendry waited a moment, but she didn't hear the sound of Jamie's footsteps going to check on the baby.

In this one area, then, she didn't have to compromise. If Sam was her baby, then she'd go check on him.

She tiptoed into the hallway, feeling like an intruder. Jamie's house was enormous. Never in her life had she lived in something with so much square footage. Her parents had sometimes bunked with friends. Kendry could remember sleeping in the back of a minivan, the Woodstock-era Volkswagen type. She'd been cozy, squashed between Mom and Dad, at least until she'd gotten older and had been to school another semester or two in America and figured out that not everyone lived that way. In fact, no one else lived that way. No one except Kendry Harrison and her wacky, hippie parents.

But as a preschooler, it had been cozy.

Would Sam ever know that kind of coziness? Never. She couldn't see herself sleeping with Jamie MacDowell, their baby tucked between them, van windows open to the night sky—

"—and the night bugs," she whispered to herself as she sank her bare toes into the plush carpet. It hadn't been that idyllic. Sam wouldn't be missing out on too much with his parents' platonic marriage.

Sam's room was next to the guest room. It was softly lit with a nightlight. There was, however, no baby in the dark wood crib. The snuffling baby sound didn't seem to come from the direction of the master bedroom at the end of the hall, either. That door was wide open, but Kendry wasn't about to tiptoe into Jamie's bedroom to check on him.

Sam was her guy, not Jamie. She wanted to find Sam.

Kendry entered the family room, her way lit by the glow of the television screen. A twenty-four-hour sports channel was on, its volume so low as to be barely noticeable. Jamie was sprawled in a brown leather recliner, all six-feet-whatever of him, sound asleep. Sam was in his arms, fussing his way into a more comfortable position against his dad's chest.

My guys. They are both mine to have and to hold, for better or worse.

She bit her lip. It didn't seem possible, but here they all were, the MacDowells. Two asleep, one awake. What was a wife and mother supposed to do in this situation?

Kendry started small. She picked up the bottle from the end table and walked it into the kitchen, then she returned to the family room. The guys looked comfortable enough. Frankly, she didn't think she'd be doing anyone a favor by picking Sam up and taking him to his crib.

Instead, she went into Jamie's bedroom and pulled a blanket from the foot of his bed, then returned to tuck it around the baby. Feeling as self-conscious as she possibly could, she lifted the edge of the blanket and pulled it down to cover Jamie's bare toes. He had nice feet, she could tell in the glow of the TV.

She felt her cheeks redden and tried to laugh at herself. She wasn't a blushing bride. She wasn't a virgin. She'd lived on a dozen beaches where people of both genders and all ages walked around half-clothed. Yet, seeing Jamie in sweatpants and bare feet felt so incredibly intimate.

I'm going to have to get over this if I'm going to live with the man for...

For how long? Had Jamie thought beyond his son's upcoming surgeries, or past Jamie's own time in the army reserves? If she was Sam's mother throughout his childhood, what would they do once Sam grew up and moved out of the house? Would they stay friends and quietly get a divorce once Sam got his college diploma?

Am I wife for a year? For a decade? Forever?

She didn't know.

Kendry turned off the TV and went to bed. Alone. In the guest room of her husband's house.

* * *

Kendry glanced at the institutional clock on the playroom wall. She only had a few minutes left on her shift, and she still hadn't found a way to tell Bailey that she'd gotten married. It was a hard thing to work into conversation.

Hey, pass me those diaper wipes, please. So, yesterday after work, I went to the courthouse with Dr. MacDowell—the E.R. one, not the cardiologist—and got married. I think Susie needs the crayons.

"I'm gonna take your temperature now," Bailey said to the preschool-aged Susie. "You don't even have to stop coloring."

As a medical assistant, Bailey had the duty to take each child's temperature. The task was a piece of cake with the latest device that let her swipe each forehead for a few seconds.

"No Sammy here this morning," Bailey said conversationally.

This was the opening Kendry needed. She liked Bailey, and she wanted to tell someone her world-changing, life-changing news. This weekend, she planned to write her parents a letter and mail it to the last tropical address they'd given her, but that wasn't the same thing at all.

"Too bad for us, huh?" Bailey continued. She wrote the child's temperature on her chart.

Kendry chickened out. "Y-yes. Sammy is my favorite."

"Sammy is everyone's favorite. If Sammy's here, we get to see his daddy at pickup time, and Daddy is definitely a favorite. Man candy. Yummy."

"I like candy," Susie announced.

"Can you draw me a picture of candy?" Bailey asked. "I know Miss Kendry likes candy, too."

Kendry pushed her taped glasses into place with one finger. "Well, I don't know about that."

Bailey waved her thermometer at Kendry. "We all like candy."

Kendry cleared her throat. "So, about Sam…"

Bailey put her hand out and grabbed Kendry's wrist. Hard. "Oh, my God."

"What is it?" Kendry looked at each child in the room, searching for the one who was in trouble.

"I'm gonna die right here. Right now. Check out the new wrapper on that candy."

Kendry turned to see a soldier approaching the playroom's glass door. He wore camouflage and walked with a purpose. He carried a baby, and when he made eye contact with Kendry through the glass, he smiled.

"I'm gonna faint," Bailey whispered.

"Me, too." Kendry covered her mouth, but it was too late. The words were out. Bailey giggled and nudged her as Jamie opened the door.

"Hi, Kendry," he said. "Are you ready to go?"

She used the fingertips covering her mouth to give him a little wave.

He handed a willing Sammy to her. Jamie greeted Bailey with a nod and a smile. In fact, Kendry thought he looked awfully smiley for a man who'd spent the night sleeping in a chair. The recliner must be comfortable.

Bailey smiled right back at Jamie. "I know Kendry is Sammy's favorite, but he and I will get along just fine when she has to leave. Don't worry about a thing, Dr. MacDowell."

Jamie glanced at Kendry with one brow raised in question. "Thanks, but Sammy and I are here to pick up Kendry. We've got some errands to run before I report for drill this weekend."

Bailey stared at Jamie for a moment. "I see."

Clearly, her tone said she did not. Kendry cleared her throat and made a halfhearted gesture toward Jamie. "I didn't get a chance to tell you yet, but Dr. MacDowell and I…kind of…got married yesterday."

Bailey stared at her. "Seriously?"

Kendry patted Sam on the back. "Yes, so I could be Sammy's mommy. He's got some surgeries coming up." Saying it out loud made it sound odd. No one got married because they had a surgery coming up.

Then Jamie took a step closer. His arm encircled her shoulders, the surprisingly smooth material of his uniform sliding across her back. The heat of his body competed with the shock on Bailey's face for Kendry's attention.

"I only had to ask her a half-dozen times," Jamie said.

"No, he didn't. Just twice." Kendry wanted to explain things to Bailey so that it all made sense, but Jamie's nearness was distracting.

"Just twice," Bailey repeated. "You got married yesterday?"

"It's not like that." Kendry stopped talking abruptly when Jamie squeezed her shoulder in a kind of warning.

"I wasn't going to let her change her mind once she finally said yes," he explained. "We eloped."

Silence followed that statement. Silence, except for the pounding of Kendry's heart. *Eloped* was such a dramatic way to describe their civil vows. Such a romantic way to describe them.

"Miss Bailey, my crayon's broken."

The child's voice seemed to break the spell Bailey was under, because she threw her arms open wide. "Well, congratulations!" She tried to close her arms around Kendry, but Sam and Jamie were there.

Bailey laughed and hugged Kendry as best she could, anyway. "Why didn't you tell me? We could have had a bachelorette party, or at least I would have bought you a cinnamon roll for a wedding cake this morning."

"Oh, I made sure she got fed this morning." The way

Jamie said it made Kendry want to drop through the floor. He made it sound like he'd fed her while she was stark naked in bed or something, when they'd really stopped at a pancake place on the way to the hospital.

Bailey gave Kendry a playful shove in the shoulder, which moved Jamie and Sam, too. "You sly thing, I didn't even know you two were dating."

For the life of her, Kendry couldn't think of a thing to say. Bailey had gotten the completely wrong impression, and Jamie had made sure she did.

Bailey made a shooing motion with her hands. "Go on, get out of here. Clock out and enjoy those *errands.*"

It took Kendry at least five minutes to think up and then discard fifty-five ways to broach the subject on her mind. Finally, she blurted it out. "Why did you do that?"

"Do what?" Jamie looked curious as he drove toward their first errand, whatever it was. Curious, and calm, and completely in control. The camouflage only made him look that much more in charge.

He looked that much more out of her league. No wonder Bailey had been so shocked.

"You made Bailey think we were really married."

"We are really married."

"I mean, like we got married because we were in love." There, she'd said it. She'd gotten that monumental word out there.

Her soldier-husband shrugged as if the L-word didn't matter. "Most people will jump to that conclusion anyway."

"I don't think they will."

That seemed to bother him a little. "Why not?"

He had to be pretending he didn't know. It was kind of him, but it was unnecessary. "We don't look like a couple. Most people don't even see me to start with, but, Jamie, look at you. You're the hottest bachelor at the hospital. You must know it." She paused deliberately, wanting him to acknowledge the truth.

He shrugged again. "Quinn doesn't know it. He thinks he's the hot one."

Kendry burst out laughing. "True enough."

Jamie pulled into a car dealership and parked. He turned in his seat to focus on her. Kendry found she couldn't hold his gaze.

She clasped her hands in her lap. "The point is, you don't have to pretend we're in love. I'm not vain. It's not going to hurt my feelings when people say how shocked they are that you married me. They'll guess that you needed someone to watch over Sam, and that's okay."

"That's not okay." Jamie placed one warm hand over her two tightly twisted ones. "As part of my family, you're important to me, and I don't want to see you get hurt. I'm not going to stand by and do nothing if someone acts shocked and you feel embarrassed."

"Bailey isn't mean. She wasn't trying to embarrass me."

"I know, but others will do it on purpose. If I can tell a true story, and believe me, it feels like I asked you a hundred times before you agreed to marry me, or if I can hold your hand and make gossip stop, then I'm going to do it."

Kendry should be firm in this. She should insist that they not pretend to anyone, because no one's opinion mattered. Jamie's plan was unnecessary.

Unnecessary, but tempting.

Jamie wanted to touch her in public. He wanted to tell people things about her that sounded romantic. She'd compromised in every area of her life, it seemed. This compromise, at least, would allow her to live a little bit of her fantasy. For a few moments at work, whenever they encountered gossip that Jamie wanted to silence, she would be treated like a woman who'd enthralled a man. Not just any man, but Dr. Jamie MacDowell, who drove a motorcycle and saved lives and wore a soldier's uniform.

She took a deep breath and looked Jamie in the eye. "If that's the way you want it, then okay."

Jamie gave her hands a brisk pat, then opened his door. "Great. Let's go get you a car."

Chapter Fourteen

In the end, of course, she compromised. She didn't want a car. Rather than tell Jamie that she didn't trust herself behind the wheel, she'd pointed out that the gossip would surely say she was a gold digger.

Jamie had countered with some disappointingly reasonable logic. "My unit drills in Dallas. I can't leave you stranded at the house all weekend. You'll need to get groceries. You'll want to go back to your place and pick up some clothes. What if Sam starts running a fever and you need to take him to the hospital?"

Kendry had let Jamie rent her a car to use while he was away. Before she signed the rental contract, she triple-checked that they'd added the optional insurance. On that, there was no compromising.

In the rental-car company's lot, Jamie pulled a large box out of the back of his truck and proceeded to install a new baby seat in the back of the rental. Then he handed her a new iPhone, showed her how to send photos with it, and told her that he, Quinn, his mother and an older brother in New York named Braden, whom she hadn't known existed, were already programmed into the speed dial. He put two hundred dollars "for groceries" into her hand, along with the keys and rental-car paperwork.

All these things he handed over to her easily. Sam took a moment longer. After a kiss on the top of his son's head and a squeeze that might have been tight enough to make Sam protest a bit, Jamie handed Kendry his son.

"I won't be gone that long," he said. "Just two nights. The time will fly."

"I know." Kendry wasn't sure if Jamie was trying to convince himself or her.

His hand drifted from the top of his son's head to her chin, as he'd done before. After lifting her face to look into her eyes, his hand drifted over her shoulder briefly, almost like he was connecting his son and his wife together in his mind with one gentle sweep of his hand.

He stepped back and nodded, then spoke in a husky voice. "Thank you. If I can't be with him, then I'm glad he's with his new mom."

He walked away. Kendry lifted Sam's hand to wave as his daddy drove off, back to the military career that had ended with a lost love and a new baby.

"He's not going to lose you, too, Sam. I'm going to take good care of you."

She drove the rental car back to Jamie's house like an actress who set the perfect example in a driver's-education movie. Considering how badly her hands were shaking once they parked in the driveway, Kendry was grateful she only dropped the car keys twice, and not the baby.

Friday night eventually became Saturday. The long, late-September Saturday turned into Sunday. As the time passed, Kendry discovered that taking care of Sam around the clock, day and night, for every feeding and for every diaper change, was...

...a joy. There was something empowering in being able to comfort a baby. Whether he needed food or a toy, whether he needed to be soothed or entertained, Kendry was able to make Sam's world better. In return, he paid attention to her like she was the center of his universe. For this weekend, she was. Sam snuggled into her like she was the most comfortable place to be.

Kendry herself couldn't remember the last time she'd been so comfortable. The shower with its modern rainfall spray was sinful, and she sinned whenever Sam napped. Her lemongrass shampoo made her hair feel almost as soft as a baby's. She'd found some disposable men's razors under the sink, so now her shaved legs were nearly as soft as Sam's, too.

The refrigerator dazzled her in stainless steel, and the ability to open the double doors wide and see shelf after shelf of brightly lit, icy-cold food was a luxury she hadn't had in years. Jamie had said they were low on food, but there were two kinds of breakfast cereals in the pantry—a pantry! A whole room just for food!—as well as a loaf of bread and a package of lunch meat in the fridge, so there was no need. She organized all the bottles of ketchup, mustard, mayonnaise, pickles.

The washing machine was the best of all, a miracle of technology after hand-scrubbing everything she owned with a bar of soap in a tiny sink. Kendry gathered up Jamie's T-shirts and sweatpants, cut the tags off the last set of her new scrubs and put everything in the machine. She pushed a few buttons and walked away. Kendry had never had this luxury.

Never. Certainly not during her childhood, living with parents who enjoyed rustic living to the extreme. Her parents had thought if they were going to learn pottery techniques from natives in a rainforest, then they should live in a wooden, thatched hut like the natives, too. When the Harrisons had returned to the States for the odd school year, beat-up Laundromats with their rusted carts and change machines had seemed the height of modern convenience.

Jamie had married her and brought her to his palace, indeed. Kendry napped, she slept, she played with Sam. She was on vacation in a luxury resort.

She only had her new scrubs to wear in the luxury resort, but that was okay. It made it easier to justify eating the man's food and showering in his house if she felt like a hired nanny in professional scrubs.

The rental car stayed in the driveway. Kendry had no desire to go to her own place and bring her old clothes into this paradise. She wanted to enjoy this fantasy a little longer. It was so much easier than deciding how to tell Jamie that his real wife had a really messed-up life.

There were some things a man shouldn't tell his mother over the phone. Jamie's marriage was bound to come as a shock, so the least he could do was tell his mother in person that he was now a married man. It would be easier to explain face-to-face why he'd taken a woman he'd known for a month to the local courthouse and bound himself to her.

Quinn gets it. Dad would have gotten it. Mom will understand when I explain it.

That's what he told himself as he traveled the last graveled piece of road that led to the River Mack Ranch. The truth was, as the grand white house came into view a few acres in the distance, he felt like a little kid about to explain to his parent that the detention slip in his backpack was not as bad as it appeared.

The ranch was located nearly an hour and a half outside of Austin. Jamie hadn't had enough time on Friday to stop by on his way to reporting to his reserve unit in Dallas. Now, on his way home, he had no excuse not to stop and reveal to his mother who, exactly, had been watching Sam for him these past few days.

He'd tell her the good news that he was married, and then he'd leave. He was impatient to get home. The entire weekend he'd been texting Kendry, and she'd been using her new iPhone to send him all the photos of Sam he could want. Her photos were funny and quirky, like a close-up of a messy baby hand along with the caption, *Where there's a will, there's a way. I can't use a spoon, but I can feed myself oatmeal.*

It had seemed natural to start sending back photos of where he was, what he was doing, whom he was with. He'd sent her a photo of the tasteless substance that passed as cake in the army's dehydrated, portable meal system, and had promised to pick up fried chicken on his way home. They'd have to pretend it didn't taste like heaven, so Sam would be content with his oatmeal while they devoured the Colonel's original recipe.

Soon. He'd be home soon. But first he had to tell his mom he had a wife. She'd obviously seen his truck coming up the road, because she was waiting on the porch, looking as if she'd been expecting company in blue slacks and a crisp white shirt. Like many Texan women of her generation, she always had her hair and makeup done, just in case.

"Well, this is a pleasant surprise," she said. "Where's the baby?"

"He's home. How are you feeling?"

"I'm fine. I could have taken care of him for you."

Jamie gave his mom an extra hug. "I'm glad to hear you're feeling up to it. Which rheumatologist did you end up seeing?"

"Oh, some new kid. He looks younger than you, and all he offered to do was run a bunch of tests."

"Mom, that's what we docs do. I'd rather he ran tests than guess why you've had these periods of weakness."

Her personal physician as well as Jamie and his brothers were all certain she had an autoimmune disease, one of those poorly understood conditions that would flare up, then nearly disappear. Just when everyone stopped fearing the monster, it would rear its ugly head and remind them that Mom was not invincible. She was getting over the worst of a flare now. Taking care of a baby all weekend would have wiped her out.

Still, she had some homemade sweet tea in a pitcher in the fridge, and she insisted on serving Jamie while he sat at her kitchen table. Affection warred with exasperation as he watched her moving a little too carefully to fill his glass with ice. "Mom, let me do that. You sit."

"I'm just fine. I can pour a glass of tea. If you'd told me you were coming, I could have had dinner in the oven, too."

"I can't stay for dinner, but I wanted to talk to you."

She set his tea down, then set herself down in the chair across from his. "Well, this sounds serious."

She looked at him with 100 percent of her attention. She'd always been like that. No matter how little he'd seen of his dad, he'd always known his mother was there for him, like Sam would now always have Kendry.

"Mom, I got married."

She blinked. "My goodness. I didn't know you were dating someone. Do I know her?"

"She works at the hospital. I think Dad would have approved."

"It sounds like you think I won't. What makes you think your father in particular would have approved?"

"Quinn approves, and he thinks like Dad. I needed a wife, and I found a woman who fit all my needs, so I didn't waste any time about it."

"It sounds more like you hired someone than like you fell in love."

"We're not in love, not the way you're thinking. But she's everything I was looking for." He used the side of his hand to make neat little karate chops on the kitchen table, punctuating each point. "She's smart. She can handle a sick child. We work together well. Done deal. Problem solved."

"What problem?" She sounded a bit faint.

"Sam needed a mother. I'm nearly as busy as Dad was. I chose the same career. I know I won't always be there for Sam. If he doesn't have a mother..." He reached across the table and touched his own mother's hand. "I can't imagine what my childhood would have been like without you."

She started to tear up. Jamie thought she was tearing up at the compliment, so her sudden disapproval caught him off guard.

"Your father was devoted to you. He loved you every bit as much as you love Sam. How can you say he wasn't there for you?"

Jamie didn't want to bring up ugly memories. He wanted to break the news that he was married, and then he wanted to go home, to the new family he was making with Sam and Kendry. "I'm sorry, Mom. Forget I said anything."

"Tell me how your father wasn't there for you."

Jamie felt his frustration build. He'd opened this can of worms. He only had himself to blame if he was late getting home. "Maybe because he missed entire football seasons when I was playing. Maybe because when he was home, he was always on the phone."

"Oh, Jamie. Have you been thinking that your whole life? Your father hated missing your games. Hated it so badly, he gave up part of his own salary to get the board to hire another physician. The board took six weeks to approve a replacement, and I thought he was going to blow a gasket at the delay. Once they got the new doctor in, your father was at every one of your games."

Jamie swallowed sweet tea as he thought back. He remembered running onto the field, completing a play, looking up at the stands, spotting his mother. Had his father been sitting right next to her? He supposed he had been, some of the time.

"I hated those camping trips." To his own ears, he sounded like a sullen adolescent.

"Oh, those camping trips." She drummed her fingers on the table, distracting the doctor in Jamie with the demonstration of dexterity that proved she was well into remission. "I tried to speak to your father about juggling his roles. We didn't have work-life balance and all those catchphrases when you were little, but we faced the same issues. Your father, though, was all or nothing. He'd realized that being near a telephone meant he was always answering calls instead of spending time with you boys. His solution was as extreme as yours."

She made little karate chops on the table, imitating him. "If the phone was a problem, then he'd take his boys where there was no phone. Problem solved."

Put that way, Jamie was uncomfortably aware that maybe Quinn wasn't the only MacDowell brother who thought like their father. Maybe Jamie tended to make decisions the same way.

He gently pressed his mother's karate hand flat on the table. "I'm having more sympathy for Dad now that I'm in his shoes. Quinn wants me to do more, to take over the medical director position from him next year, or at least chair the emergency department. But every career yes is a Sam no."

"Did you decide to say yes to the career? Is that why you married someone, to gain a full-time nanny for Sam? I don't think you should criticize your father, then. Your solution is more extreme than anything he ever came up with, and

it puts work before family, which he never willingly did."
She stood abruptly.

Jamie stood, too, defensive and more emotional than he
wanted to be. "That's not why I got married. I'm still refusing to take on more work, because I want to spend every
minute I can with Sam. Marrying Kendry wasn't extreme.
It was rational."

"Your father didn't marry me because it was rational. He
married me for love. Crazy, passionate love."

Jamie winced. "Mom, please."

"It's true. You need that in your life."

"I had that in my life. How do you think Sam came
about?"

The memories came back to him in a rush, vivid and emo-
tional, now that he'd opened the door a crack to discuss earlier days. He saw Amina clearly, dark eyes flashing, daring
him to take everything she had to give. He covered his eyes
with his hand and waited for the wave to pass.

It took a moment to be able to breathe again. "I will never,
ever love anyone the way I loved Amina."

His mother hugged him. "I'm sorry, son. I don't want you
to settle for anything less than that."

Jamie took a deep breath, dropped his hand, blinked at
the kitchen he'd grown up in. "Yes, well, *that* is gone. I'll
never feel for another woman that way."

His mother frowned. "Not that precise way, no. But that
doesn't mean you'll never fall in love again." She pushed
Jamie into the chair she'd been in, then pulled out the chair
next to him. She put her hand on his knee. "The longer you
stay married to this girl, the easier it will be for her to win
alimony. Your share of this ranch could become hers, if her
lawyer is good enough. Will she put up a fight, or can you
end this quickly and quietly?"

Jamie froze at the thought of losing Kendry.

No.

All his earlier caveman instincts came back, full force. He'd lost Amina. No way in hell was he going to lose Kendry. He needed her, and she was his now. His.

"I'm not ending my marriage. Ever."

"Oh." His mother let go of him immediately, as if she'd gotten an electric shock. "I thought you married a girl you weren't passionate about."

"She's not a girl. She's my wife, and she doesn't want this ranch. She doesn't know it exists." His mother was so off base, it was laughable. So, Jamie tried to laugh.

"Tell me about her, then."

"What do you want to know?"

"You could start with her name."

"Kendry Harrison." And then, because he'd learned the information on the marriage license, and because his mother was still looking at him strangely, he told her more. "Kendry Ann Harrison. She'll turn twenty-four in December. That might sound young, but she grew up all over the world. She's seen a lot. We eat lunch together, which is usually the only bright spot of sanity in my workday. There are times at that hospital when I'd swear Kendry is the only person I can talk to, the only person who gets me."

His mother was silent.

Way to go. Way to hurt your mother's feelings.

Tiredly, Jamie stood. His mother stood, too, using the table for leverage. Jamie saw tears in her eyes. They might have been from pain because her joints had stiffened while she sat, but he feared it was worse than that. He'd made her sad.

"Don't cry, Mom. Please, I didn't mean it that way. I know I can always talk to you, too."

She accepted his hug, resting her head briefly on his shoulder. "Oh, I hope you did mean it, son. I hope this woman is the one who understands you. It's very special when you find someone who doesn't try to change you."

She stepped back, keeping her hands on Jamie's arms, and gave him a little shake. "So tell me, is she pretty?"

Jamie rolled his eyes. "I can't tell you how sick I am of people talking about her appearance. She loves Sam. That's what matters."

His mother only raised an eyebrow at him. He could practically see the wheels turning in her head. She'd never reminded him more of Braden.

Aw, damn it. Braden. He'd forgotten to tell Braden he was married. That was going to have to happen by phone. Jamie wasn't going to fly to Manhattan when there wasn't a thing Braden could say that would make him change his mind about Kendry.

Kendry. He wanted to go home, to his house, to his wife, to his child. Now.

"Okay, Mom. The top of her head comes to about here on me." With the side of his hand, he touched his jaw. "She's got brown hair, and she wears glasses that make her eyes look kind of hazel. But when she doesn't have them on, if you brush her bangs away, her eyes are actually green. She's waiting for me, Mom, so I've got to go now."

His mother didn't move, except to tilt her head a little as she continued to study him.

"She's waiting for me. So…okay?"

"Okay. Go home to your green-eyed wife, then. I can't wait to meet her." His mother walked him outside to his truck. She seemed pretty happy now, and Jamie was relieved enough that he wasn't going to question why.

He hadn't backed up his truck five feet, however, when his mother waved at him to stop.

She leaned in the window, one hand on the ledge like she'd keep the truck in place that way. "You let me know when you're coming with her. None of this dropping by without giving a person notice. Not when I'm meeting my new daughter-in-law for the first time. I've got to have a cake ready at the very least."

"Yes, Mom."

"You promise?"

"I promise."

Jamie breathed in the late-afternoon air as he drove down the ranch road, watching the familiar scenery of his childhood roll by. He was exhausted by the conversation. Exhausted by the whole weekend. Yet he was leaving here with less anger toward the memory of his father, and a strange feeling that his mother agreed that the detention slip in his backpack wasn't so awful after all.

Chapter Fifteen

Kendry heard Sammy wake up with his usual cry. Not a cry of distress, but the one she thought sounded like he was saying, "Hey, I'm bored in here. Come and get me."

"I'm coming, my little alarm clock," she muttered to herself as she stretched briefly in bed. She felt great after another night of satiated sleep, this time with a belly full of fried chicken.

Kendry swung her legs over the side of the bed and stood up, marveling as she did every morning at how rich the plush carpet felt under her arches. She tugged Jamie's T-shirt into place and walked into Sammy's room with her eyes still half-closed.

Jamie was already there, wearing his sweatpants. Nothing else. His back was to her as he bent over the crib, and the movement of his shoulder muscles under an acre of smooth, male skin penetrated her sleep-fogged brain in the most delicious way.

He's got no shirt on, because I'm wearing it. It was a silly thought, of course. Jamie must own dozens of T-shirts, yet it seemed as if between the two of them, they were sharing one outfit. He was bare on top. She was bare on the bottom.

Her eyes popped open. She was really, really bare on the bottom. She tugged the hem of his shirt another inch lower on her thighs at the moment he turned around with the baby in his arms. "Good morning," he said, flashing her an easy, friendly smile, clearly oblivious to her state of undress.

She only had one pair of underwear in the house, the pair she'd been wearing when Jamie had whisked her away from the city bus stop on his motorcycle. Every night, she'd been washing them and putting them in the dryer. Every morning, wearing nothing but the man's T-shirt, she'd gone into the laundry room and put the freshly cleaned pair back on. No big deal, to sleep in a T-shirt only.

Only today, the T-shirt's owner was standing three feet away from her, smiling, and she felt practically naked. He *looked* practically naked.

Kendry started backing out of the room, tugging the front of the T-shirt down while she swore she felt a breeze on her bare backside. "Yes, um, good morning. I'll just, uh, go get ready, since you've got Sam."

She backed up into the hallway bathroom and shut the door. Her heart was pounding. Her face felt hot. She glanced in the mirror. The T-shirt came all the way down to the middle of her thighs. Jamie couldn't possibly have seen whether or not she was wearing underwear. She should have been more worried about her hair, which was falling in an uncombed pillow-mess down to her shoulders.

It only took a few moments to go through her morning routine. Teeth brushed, face washed, hair brushed and ponytail holder twisted into service, she cracked the door open again, hoping to get into the laundry room and back to her bedroom without any more awkward *good mornings*.

She stepped into the hall when the silence was interrupted by the unmistakable sound of the washing machine lid being opened. Good lord. The man did his laundry first thing in the morning. Kendry hurried through the kitchen toward the laundry room.

"Wait," she called. "I'll get my things."

Too late. The release mechanism for the clothes dryer's door made a distinctive noise. Kendry jogged the last steps into the laundry room. There Jamie stood, in all his bare-chested glory, with a handful of wet camouflage clothing in one hand and, in his other arm, a baby who was using his father's naked shoulder as a teething ring. Jamie was staring in the dryer.

"Here, let me get my stuff." Kendry nearly elbowed him out of the way. Sure enough, although she'd thrown her bath towel in with her unmentionables, her bra and underwear rested on top, in plain view. She snatched the clothes and held them to her front. "Sorry."

"Sorry," Jamie said at the same time. He gestured with the wet clothes in his hand. "Thought I'd get these uniforms washed before work."

"Sure. My stuff's all done." Kendry retreated to her bedroom and didn't emerge until she was fully dressed. Fully. From her old bra and underwear to her new socks and scrubs. Sneakers on, laces tied. Completely dressed.

When she walked into the kitchen, she saw that Jamie was dressed, too, in boots and slacks and a dress shirt. She seized the opportunity to talk about anything except laundry. "You're expecting a slow day today, aren't you? On nights and weekends, you wear scrubs."

"You are one very observant wife." Jamie had placed Sam in a bouncy chair and was shaking up a bottle of formula. He was an efficient man, all right. She supposed he'd had no choice, being a single parent.

He looked over his shoulder at her. "You're wearing your wedding scrubs."

"I guess they are, aren't they?" Kendry was wearing the pink pair that had set off her tears the day they'd gotten married. Her old glasses were firmly in place, still serviceable until the new ones came in.

"I didn't realize you had to work today." Jamie checked his watch. "What time does your shift start?"

"I'm off. I kind of assumed I'd be home with Sammy." They should have discussed this over fried chicken. Instead, they'd told each other amusing stories about their separate weekends.

"I think Sam wants to be with you whether you are in the playroom or at home." Jamie sat Sam upright in his lap and started to give him his bottle. "If you don't have to go to the hospital today, why are you in scrubs?"

"They're comfortable." Kendry had been wearing his T-shirt and her scrub pants when he'd gotten home the night before, and Jamie had jumped to the conclusion that she'd gotten ready for bed early.

"You never went back to your place this weekend, did you? Not even to get some clothes?"

"No, I didn't feel like it."

Jamie seemed thoughtful as he watched Sam drink his bottle. "You didn't go to the grocery store, either. We're out of bread and cereal."

"I'm sorry. I should have saved you some for breakfast today."

"That's not the problem, Kendry. I can grab something at the hospital. The problem is, what are you going to eat for breakfast if you're not going to work today?"

"Oh, don't worry about me. We've got mashed potatoes left over from last night."

Jamie sighed, then stayed silent.

Kendry bit her lip. It was hard to read his thoughts as he watched Sam finish his bottle, but Jamie clearly wasn't relaxed or happy or any of the things she wanted him to be now that they were married.

"I like mashed potatoes," she said. "Honest."

Jamie looked up at her. "The real problem is trying to figure out why you stayed in this house for two and a half days. Do you feel like it's not your place to use the money I gave you for groceries?"

Surprise made her hesitate. "I can do the grocery shopping if you tell me what you like. Do you want the same brand of cereal again?"

"You live here now. This is your house. You should buy your favorite cereal, not only mine."

"I can't just barge in here and take over. That's not the way I am."

The corner of his mouth lifted. "That's too much the way I am. Last time we went to a store together, I took over. As I recall, my wife didn't appreciate it." Jamie put the empty bottle down and started patting Sam's back. He kept his eyes on her, however. "Tell me the truth, Kendry. How badly do you hate to drive?"

Dang it.

She gave up and sat down. "Really badly."

"There's no bus stop around here. I'll drive to the grocery store, but you have to take a few laps around the empty part of the parking lot so that you get more comfortable behind the wheel. Deal?"

Her little fantasy weekend in the castle was over.

"Deal."

The compromising resumed.

Jamie was pouring himself a cup of coffee in the E.R.'s kitchenette when it hit him. He'd bought her scrubs and he'd bought her socks, but he hadn't bought Kendry any underwear. Underpants. Panties. Whatever the hell they were, there had been one clean pair in the dryer, one scrap of pale blue, plain cotton, which meant—

He shoved the stainless-steel pot back onto the burner. So, she slept commando. When she'd been standing there in Sammy's room, with her hair loose and her glasses gone, she'd been bare-assed under his shirt. He hadn't thought about it at the time. He'd only been surprised by how fluffy her hair was when it wasn't scraped back in a ponytail.

But Kendry had been aware of it. Their odd tango in the laundry room, the way she'd backed out of Sammy's room with quick, small steps, it all made sense now.

It was funny, really. An amusing little bit between room-mates.

Jamie didn't feel like laughing. He had a sudden vision, a piece of a remembered dream, of a woman's legs silhouetted against the glow of the television and a blanket drifting down over his feet. The memory was uncomfortable. Almost erotic.

"How's married life treating you?" Quinn's big voice crashed into Jamie's thoughts.

He grunted at Quinn, took a sip of his coffee. "Did you come here on my bike or in your truck?"

Quinn reached across him for the coffeepot. "It's *my* bike. If you want to buy it back, it'll cost you. But I've got the truck today."

"Good. I need you to help me move Kendry's stuff into my house."

Quinn took out his phone and flipped through a few screens. "I can make Wednesday a half day."

"Tonight. She needs clothes."

"You sure about that? This is your honeymoon, after all." Quinn leaned against the counter with his coffee and looked like he was settling in to enjoy a series of jabs.

Jamie pitched his voice low, conscious now of eavesdropping staff. "It's not like that, and you know it. She needs her own clothes. She can't keep wearing mine—and don't try raising that eyebrow at me like Dad."

A nurse peeked in the kitchenette. "Dr. MacDowell? We've got an MI on the way. Two minutes. Radio says he coded."

Jamie set down his coffee, tamed the adrenaline rush as he headed toward the room they kept ready for the most serious cases and tried not to feel too grateful for the distraction.

"Six o'clock?" Quinn called after him.

"Six. Thanks."

Chapter Sixteen

Kendry was back in her old neighborhood. Despite her objections, Jamie was with her, driving the pickup truck that he erroneously thought was needed to move all of her belongings from her place to his.

He'd even come home tonight with Quinn and a second truck, as if she needed a convoy of pickups to haul all her worldly possessions. Quinn had been pressed into babysitting Sammy instead.

"Are you sure Sammy's okay with Quinn?" Kendry asked. "Make a left here."

Jamie flicked on the turn signal. "He can thread a wire into a man's heart. He can tape a disposable diaper over a baby's bottom."

One more left turn, and they were there. Kendry's home. Her heart sank as she tried to see it for the first time, the way Jamie was seeing it. The driveway they parked on was choked with weeds, and the bushes grew wild all around the dingy home exterior. The house still stood despite the neglect, probably because it had been built of brick.

When Kendry had found this neighborhood, she'd noticed how sturdy the block of brick houses were and had thought it a point in their favor. She'd had no choice but to overlook the signs of neglect, the furniture left to rot in the front yards, the chain-link fences allowed to rust away. Kendry was glad she'd swung that machete to tame the foreclosed house's weeds not long ago. The street looked better for it.

"This is your house?" Jamie's voice was obviously, painfully, neutral. Nonjudgmental, when there was only one judgment possible. Kendry's heart squeezed in her chest in gratitude.

"I rent the garage, actually."

The truck cab felt stifling, the air thick with silence. There was nothing Jamie could say without making her feel worse, and he probably knew it.

She took her glasses off and looked out the window. It was nearly seven, and people were starting to loiter in the streets. During the day, the place was a ghost town, but at night, people came out of their houses. Neighbors started sharing beers, laughingly taunting one another. It took a few hours for the camaraderie to turn vicious. Kendry didn't leave the safety of her brick-walled garage at night.

"I should have used the rental car and moved my stuff out myself. I didn't want to bring Sam here, I guess." *Not even in the daylight.*

Jamie opened his truck door. "Come out on my side. That bush is blocking your door." He gave her hand a tug as she slid across the bench seat. Once she was out, he didn't let go while he used his free hand to grab an empty cardboard box out of the truck bed. They crunched their way over rocks and weeds toward the garage's side door.

Inside, the temperature was easily over a hundred degrees. Kendry tucked her taped glasses into the breast pocket of her scrubs. She lowered the half window on the door and turned on her little electric fan. "This will cool things off. It's amazing how much a fan helps."

"I know. It was the same way in Afghanistan." Jamie dropped the box onto the concrete floor. "We should put the bigger stuff in the truck first, like that chest of drawers."

"The furniture isn't mine. The apartment came furnished." She'd always called it her apartment. It had a tiny, dorm-sized fridge and an electric hot plate, so she had a kitchen. The twin bed and chest of drawers were her bedroom. It was just a quick hop across the yard to the utility room of Mrs. Haines's house, which had a sink, toilet and microscopic shower stall. All the components of an apartment were here.

"Did you write to your parents yet?" Jamie's question was unexpected.

"No. Why do you ask?" Kendry pulled open the lowest drawer and took out her favorite sweatshirt, which was wrapped around one of her parents' pottery pieces, and set it carefully in the box.

Nearly done packing.

Jamie was still on the topic of her parents. "I need to find a way to send them money without offending them. We could fly them back to the States under the pretense of celebrating our marriage. I've got enough to help get them on their feet, if they want to live here."

"Get them on their feet? Jamie, my parents aren't poor." He went very still. "Don't tell me they have money."

"They have all they want. They're fine."

"They're fine," he repeated in his flat voice. Suddenly, he shoved her one and only chair away with his boot. "Then what the hell is this? Some kind of sink-or-swim lesson? They cut you loose to live on your own in a gang neighborhood?"

"I'm almost twenty-four years old, Jamie. I'm not their

responsibility." Pride made her pretend she was the proud owner of this place. "It may not look like much to you, but I'm really doing fine."

"This neighborhood is dangerous. You've been starving. What kind of parents let their child starve if they have money?"

"They're good parents, Jamie. I came back to the States with money for college and everything. It wasn't their fault I blew it, so I haven't asked them for more." She sank onto the end of her bed while Jamie paced one lap around her one-car garage.

He returned to the bed and sat next to her. "If they're good parents, they have no idea about what part of Austin you live in, do they?"

Kendry shook her head. "It's only temporary, so why worry them? It might take me eight years, but I'm going to be a college graduate with a nursing degree. The end result will be the same."

"What happened to your college fund? You're the most responsible person I know. Were you robbed?"

Kendry shook her head.

"Were you in over your head, involved with a bad crowd? Drugs?"

"No."

Jamie would find out everything, sooner or later. If they were still married on September thirtieth, she couldn't keep it a secret. She stood and walked to the door. The fan pushed the hot air past her, out the window she'd been so proud to rent. Even the view of overgrown shrubs had brought her pleasure, because they were an improvement over her previous circumstances.

Jamie's opinion of her had always mattered. Maybe she could make him see how much progress she'd made on her own. But first, she had to tell him how stupid she'd been.

"We were never rich, but during the times we lived in the

States, we usually rented a real apartment. We had a TV. I had shoes. My parents wouldn't have let me wear worn-out sneakers, either." She looked down at her new sneakers and flexed her foot.

"And then?" Jamie stayed on the bed, giving her his full attention.

"And then I got my GED right before I turned twenty. Finally. The diploma arrived while we were living in Mexico. My high school years were mostly spent overseas, so I got too old to keep enrolling whenever we came back for a few months. It's embarrassing to be an eighteen-year-old sophomore. Anyway, when the GED arrived, my parents surprised me with this nest egg they'd saved for me. They left Mexico for Peru, and I came to Austin, ready to enroll in the community college."

"Why Austin?"

"I'd made friends who were from here, people my age who were vacationing in Mexico." Kendry remembered their fun-loving confidence. She was an American high school grad, too, like they were—or so she'd reasoned.

"I moved in with two of them, sharing rent on a great house. Three bedrooms and a swimming pool in a gated community. The guy had one bedroom, which he shared with his girlfriend. The girl had one bedroom, which she shared with her boyfriend. I had the third all to myself. The four of them got me a part-time job where they worked. I was thrilled to be waitressing at this high-end, trendy restaurant, bringing home hundreds in tips.

"My share of the rent was in the hundreds, too, though. I did the math and decided if I worked full-time, I could keep living with my friends and save a little more for college, as well. If I worked for two semesters instead of going to school, then I'd have enough to skip community college and go straight to a university for all four years."

"Knowing you, it was probably a solid plan."

"I kept pushing that college entry back. I decided I could buy a car if I worked for three semesters, and then go to university." She rested against the doorjamb, watching the shrubs blow in the evening breeze. It was nearly dark outside, and she tried to remember if Jamie had locked the truck.

"The guy and the girl decided they loved each other instead of their roommates, and they ran off. I was left with a weeping ex-girlfriend and an angry ex-boyfriend who didn't want to pay their share of the rent. After a week, the two of them had a fight. They broke a window. I thought I'd been robbed, until the girl returned to get her clothes. She left. He left. I was alone when the bills for the month came in. Electric. Water. Satellite. Internet. Rent."

She kept her arms wrapped around her stomach, feeling sick at the memory. There'd been so many bills, arriving in the mail one after another.

"Half my savings were wiped out in one month. Half. Then a new restaurant opened up, and our trendy place stopped being trendy. Within a week, my tips plummeted from hundreds to tens. No one I knew could afford to move in with me."

She wanted Jamie to understand. It had all been one domino falling after another, one huge downward spiral. "I panicked when the rent was due again. Four weeks came so fast. I let my car insurance lapse to pay the bills, but then I got in an accident. I rear-ended a car. I got the ticket."

"And you got the medical bills?" Jamie sat forward on the bed and rubbed his face with his hands. "God, Kendry. How long were you in the hospital?"

"Not a minute, thankfully. I wasn't going fast enough to trigger the air bags, but I'd hit the other car at a little bit of angle, they told me. Just enough to throw the frame out of whack. I totaled a Mercedes."

Jamie frowned at that.

Kendry was getting used to him frowning at her now that they were married, but she didn't like it. He'd always been so nice to her when they were just friends, talking to her easily over cafeteria lunches, listening to her stories. Of course, she hadn't told him stories like this one.

She went back to staring out the window. "It's that easy to go from having a little bit of savings to using the public library's free computer to look up homeless shelters."

"You lived in a homeless shelter," he repeated in that carefully neutral voice, the voice that didn't fool her. There was only one judgment to make.

"Look, I know it was a stupid gamble, to go for a month without car insurance. You know the law in Texas. If you break it, you have to pay for it, whether you have car insurance or not. That's fair, but it hasn't been easy. For two years, I've been buying a Mercedes-Benz, one paycheck at a time. I've got twelve payments to go. I'll make the next payment on September thirtieth."

"The judge expected you to pay off a Mercedes in three years?" In the corner of her eye, she saw Jamie stand up. "Kendry, most people who buy a Mercedes get a loan that lasts far longer than thirty-six months. Did you appeal?"

"Appeal what? I hit them from behind."

"Your sentence was outrageous."

Kendry had nothing to say to that. She'd been living with it so long, it seemed normal to her. "The good news is, the thirtieth is also my six-month anniversary at the hospital. I'll have health insurance for the first time in my life, and I get a raise. Another fifty cents per hour."

Outside, a bird twittered near her window. People called out to each other across the street.

A single gunshot rang out.

Jamie tackled her. His arms came around her as he landed with her on the ground, hard. Her head would have bounced off the concrete had he not cradled it in his hand. She gasped into his neck, tasted the salt of his skin as she panted in fear.

"A car," she breathed, as soon as she was able. "A car backfired. S'okay."

He was heavy on her, clasping her to his chest. "It's gunfire." He rolled off just enough to slide them both closer to the brick wall, away from the wooden door.

"No, I've heard that sound before. People have old cars around here, and they backfi—"

Several gunshots sounded, a dozen within a second, sounding like an automatic machine gun. A woman screamed. Kendry was instantly smashed underneath Jamie again.

Long moments passed. Outside, everything had gone utterly silent. No birds. No people. Inside, she could hear only her own heart pounding in her ears, her own shallow, rapid breathing. She wanted to take a deeper breath, but Jamie was holding her too tightly. His breathing seemed steady and even, but her face was pressed against his neck, and she could feel his pulse, strong and quick.

"You're right," she panted. "That was gunfire."

Jamie didn't say anything, and she remembered his earlier comment about Afghanistan. Perhaps he was going through a kind of post-traumatic stress episode. Concerned, and more than a little shaken herself, she lifted her hand and combed her fingers through his hair. "Jamie? Are you okay?"

He eased up far enough to look into her face. Their breaths mingled. "You've heard that sound before?"

She nodded, feeling very small and very inexperienced in the arms of a man who'd lived through a war.

"And what did you do? Did you lie there on your bed, telling yourself it was a car? A bullet could have shattered that glass. You could have been killed where you lay. How could I protect you from that?"

Kendry recognized the look in his eyes, the slightly wild

look he'd had in the emergency room when he'd talked about Amina and Sammy and her. About the responsibility he felt. About the normalcy he craved. She felt like she'd deceived him, agreeing to marry him when she'd known all along that she would add to his burdens, not lighten them.

"You don't have to protect me."

"The hell I don't."

"I'm not stupid. I wouldn't just lie there if bullets were flying."

He gave her a little shake, his face so close she felt the air vibrate with his voice. "Bullets *were* flying. You stood by the window."

"You didn't give me a chance to move!" She wasn't helpless. She wasn't a mess. She'd worked damned hard to live in these brick walls.

The wind had been knocked out of her by the man who was even now squeezing her too tightly, smashing her glasses into her breast. She'd been lying on the floor long enough for the concrete to start hurting her shoulder and hip. She wriggled, pushing at his arms, but he was too big for her to budge.

"Let me up." Tears of frustration filled her eyes. "This hurts."

It was the wrong thing to say. Or maybe it was the right thing. He rolled to his side, taking his weight off her. As she took a deep breath, he started running his hand over her arm, her waist, her leg.

"I'm okay," Kendry said, but his hand wasn't quite steady, not quite the touch of a doctor. He smoothed his way clumsily up her ribs, brushed the side of her breast. She inhaled quickly.

"It hurts where?" Jamie said roughly. She couldn't take her eyes off him, the way his lips were firm, the way the muscles in his neck were tight with tension.

"Just—no. My glasses were in the way—"

His fingers were on her breast, dipping into her pocket, pulling out her glasses. He tossed the taped frames away. As they skittered across the concrete, his hand returned to her breast, fully cupping her this time, hot and sure, sliding his thumb over the peak in a single, experienced stroke.

Her gasp was captured by Jamie's mouth as he kissed her, one searing meeting of his mouth on hers. Her thoughts froze, until Jamie parted her lips, tasting her fully, and Kendry came alive in a burst of sensation. She whimpered with need, overwhelmed by the rush of want.

He pressed his hand, his mouth, his whole body into her. She melted underneath him, hotly returning his kiss.

Abruptly, he rolled away.

Kendry lay on the floor, panting for air, feeling dazed and alone. She wasn't aware of Jamie sitting up, but his strong arms lifted her by the shoulders, and then she was cradled with her back against his chest.

"My fault," he murmured into her hair. "My fault. Forgive me. I should never have…not with you."

Not with her? Not with his wife, who loved him terribly? *Then with whom?*

She wanted to howl the question, but the answer came to her too quickly.

With Amina.

The gunfire. The desire to protect a civilian. Beyond a doubt, it all had combined in his mind with yesterday's military training to remind him of Amina, Sam's mother. Sam's real mother.

Kendry was, and always would be, second best for Jamie. This kiss had changed nothing.

She'd married him for one reason: to make a family for Sam. As awful as it was, Sam had never known Amina. Unlike his father, Sam didn't miss Amina, but he would miss Kendry if she walked away.

I would miss him, my favorite little guy. I'd miss both of my guys.

She couldn't jeopardize this marriage and her chance at motherhood.

She dashed her tears away and blew the bangs out of her eyes. She smiled brightly at the mattress of her bed, just to get her facial muscles working, then turned around to face Jamie.

"No big deal," she said.

Jamie seemed a little startled at her chipper tone.

"You were remembering Amina, I know. If all the soldiers who returned from war kissed the way you do, then I don't think there'd be so much research into post-traumatic stress disorder right now." She patted his shoulder and stood up. "Let's get my stuff and go. We still need to hit the grocery store."

Chapter Seventeen

Jamie knew he'd broken the rules. He'd crossed the line. He'd mauled Kendry on the floor of her old apartment, and she'd forgiven him on the spot for mistaking her for Amina.

The hell of it was, he hadn't been thinking of Amina. Not for one second. He'd known full well it was Kendry in his arms. Everything about her was different than Amina, from the shape of her to the scent of her skin and the taste of her mouth. He'd known it was Kendry he was kissing. Kendry he wanted to toss on the bed.

Four weeks had passed, and it was still Kendry he wanted in his bed.

If she knew, she'd hate him. She admired him for staying devoted to Amina. She'd married him only after he'd promised her that his feelings were buried.

They were.

This wasn't love. It was lust, an unfortunate part of that caveman satisfaction he felt toward all things Kendry. It was undeniably gratifying to watch the changes marriage made in his wife. She no longer sneezed and sniffed. The dark circles under her eyes were gone, and her new glasses with their barely there frames let her look at the world without squinting. She was no longer gaunt, but fit and slender. The doctor in him appreciated how healthy she now looked.

The caveman in him did not appreciate how the other doctors looked at her, but Jamie buried that emotion with grim determination. Jealousy. Lust. Love. He would allow none of them to destroy what he had with Kendry.

Sam was blossoming in the new family they were making. Between Kendry's personal history and her true interest in medicine, Jamie understood why she hadn't wanted to quit her hard-won job at the hospital, but he'd been touched when she cut her hours down to one day per week. On most days, Jamie came home to find her on a blanket on the floor with Sam. Sam had started crawling, early for a premature baby. All that blanket time with Kendry was paying off.

Jamie would be a fool to lose everything for the sake of a purely physical tumble with Kendry. She'd think less of him for betraying Amina, and she would be right to think so. How could he love another woman, when he'd loved Amina?

Jamie would leave the blanket time to Sam. If the phrase conjured visions of a tousled Kendry amid tangled blankets on his bed, that was his personal problem. He would never risk his family for something purely physical.

The anxiety Kendry felt during Sam's first surgery made her feel like a real mother. The threat of pneumonia had passed, and Sam's doctors had decided to repair the hole in his heart first. It was, as Jamie had warned her on their wedding day, not easy when a child she loved was scared and in pain.

The repair was a relatively simple procedure, performed in the cardiac cath lab. A wire was threaded through an artery, then positioned over the hole between the upper chambers of the heart. Between beats, a patch was unfurled through the same wire and set in place over the hole, where it stuck by the force of pressure within the heart itself. Within months, Kendry was told, the heart tissue would grow over the patch, making the repair permanent.

To Kendry, it was a miracle. To her husband and her brother-in-law, it was routine. Still, Jamie held her hand during the two-hour wait, and she knew that it wasn't a ploy to silence the hospital gossips.

He took a few days off to be with Sam during his recovery, holding Sam most of the time to limit his activity for the first forty-eight hours. Jamie did everything himself, even turning down Kendry's offer to change Sam's diaper.

"I want my son to know I'm always here for him," Jamie explained.

"You make changing a diaper sound very noble," she joked in response, but for the first time, Kendry started to wonder if it was a bit obsessive. By the third day, Kendry realized Jamie stuck like glue to Sam because he had nothing else to do.

She didn't, either, so she decided to tackle the stack of boxes that prevented them from parking the truck in the garage. She'd expected to uncover winter clothes, or perhaps a kitchen gadget. Instead, she discovered mementos that revealed the man Jamie had been before she'd met him. A whole life existed in the boxes, one that Jamie had evidently packed up before leaving for Afghanistan. One he had never picked up again.

"I didn't know you rode horses," she said over dinner, watching Jamie patiently spoon mushed-up bananas into Sam's mouth.

"I don't anymore. Sam's too young."

After dinner, Kendry brought in a framed football-team photo. Jamie was the team doctor, crouched in the front row with the coaches. The team had written thanks for his volunteer work in black marker. "We should hang this some-where. Who is the team doctor now?"

Jamie looked at the photo like it had nothing to do with him. "One of the kids' dads took over when I was deployed."

She found a motorcycle helmet and snowboard gear.

Jamie had nothing to do with any of it.

The Jamie she knew returned to work the next day, then came home and cared for Sam. The Jamie she knew had never done anything else.

In his quest to be a great father, he'd given up too much. He was expecting Sam to fulfill all his needs. That couldn't be good for him, or for Sam. No baby, no matter how cher-ished, could meet an adult's every social, mental and emo-tional need.

In fact, Kendry was feeling a little stir-crazy herself. She couldn't hire a babysitter, though, and take her husband on a date. As nice as her new mother-in-law had been when they'd visited with Sam, Kendry couldn't ask her to watch the baby for a weekend while she took her husband snow-boarding in nearby New Mexico.

They didn't have that kind of marriage.

She was, however, the only wife Jamie had. Like a mil-lion wives before her, she decided it was time to manage her husband—for his own good.

Kendry decided to start small: a family outing to a high school football game. Quinn had told her he'd never seen Jamie take Sam anywhere except their mother's house. It was appalling to her that the people who'd known Jamie his whole life hadn't met his son yet. If she'd had this adorable baby, she'd want everyone to meet him.

"Easy-peasy, lemon-squeezy," Kendry sang to Sam as she snapped the bottom of a red Onesie over his fresh dia-per. The high school's colors were red, white and blue, so Kendry added blue overalls to complete Sam's school spirit outfit. "What's the point of having a gorgeous baby like you if we don't get to show you off? Your daddy is going to bask in your reflected glory tonight."

Jamie was going to enjoy fatherhood, by golly, and Kendry was going to make sure of it, even if she had to kidnap him tonight to do it. Unfortunately, she was pretty sure she that was exactly what she was going to have to do.

Kendry buckled Sam into his car seat and headed the truck toward the hospital to pick up Jamie, doubt assailing her every mile of the way. She was more nervous to take Jamie to a football game than she'd been to marry him. She'd been certain Jamie wanted to marry her. She wasn't at all sure what he would do when she drove him to his alma mater's stadium.

Of course, showing off his son meant Jamie would be introducing his wife to old friends, as well. How many times at the hospital had Jamie put his arm around her shoulders, silently defending her when any member of the hospital staff raised their eyebrows in surprise that she—plain Kendry Harrison—was his wife? How many times had Jamie repeated his "Sam and I like you just the way you are" line?

She was supposed to be lightening Jamie's load, not adding to the burden. Superficial or not, having people think his wife looked pitiful was, well, pitiful. The new glasses helped, of course, and at the hospital, everyone wore scrubs, so that was a certain equalizer. But this morning, as she'd stood in front of the bathroom mirror, scissors in hand, ready to trim her bangs for tonight's outing, she'd wondered if there was more to her routine than being thrifty and frugal. Perhaps she was being plain stubborn, refusing to change because she was too proud. Perhaps it had been easier these past two years to pretend that everyone else was shallow, rather than that she had fallen into poverty.

She tossed the scissors down and picked up the phone. She wasn't doing Jamie any favors by sticking to her old routine. It was hard to spend someone else's money on herself, but in this case, she was spending it to make Jamie's night a little less stressful. That made all the difference.

It was amazing how easy some things were to accomplish once she set her mind to it. Bailey had answered the phone, and Kendry had arrived at Bailey's stylist within two hours. Sam had reveled in cooing female attention while Kendry let the stylist have his way. He'd cut long layers into the rest of Kendry's hair to blend it with the long bangs, gushing about "sexy beach waves" the whole time.

Kendry's experiences with beaches were that they were sandy and left her hair a tangled mess, but when the stylist had turned her toward the mirror to see the final result, she'd decided to skip her ponytail for the evening. She looked like the carefree coed who'd worn a mini while waitressing in the latest Austin hot spot. Kendry had almost forgotten that person.

Now, sitting in the truck, waiting at the last red light before the hospital, Kendry fluffed and finger-combed her hair. Maybe Jamie meant it each time he said he liked her just the way she was. Maybe he didn't want Sam's new mother to look different. When he said she should spend money on herself, maybe he meant on her education, not on something frivolous like a hairdo.

Enough. The money had been spent. The damage, so to speak, was done.

The light turned green. She'd find out what her husband thought soon enough.

Chapter Eighteen

As soon as she saw Jamie headed from the E.R.'s ambulance entrance toward the truck, Kendry's heart sped up. As usual, he'd changed from scrubs to jeans. The October air was crisp in the evening, so he wore his leather jacket. He looked like a movie star with his military haircut, handsome, tall and strong. Memories of that hot kiss on the floor were never far away.

Stop it.

Her husband was her friend, a caring man, one who'd given her that same jacket to wear for her own safety. He was devoted to his son. Knowing Sam was in this E.R. without him had torn him up that day.

Jamie flashed a quick smile as he came up to the truck door, and Kendry was right back to square one: her husband looked like a movie star. Her *platonic* husband, the devoted father…

Lord, she needed to keep it all straight.

"Hi." She waved as Jamie walked up and opened her door.

She gripped the steering wheel and delivered her first, carefully constructed line. "Why don't you let me drive tonight? You look tired."

He actually looked very alert at the moment, openly checking out her clothes. She'd spent a little more money on herself in that department, too. Football in Texas was big, an Institution with a capital *I*. Her new red sweater, worn over a good pair of jeans and boots, would take her anywhere in Austin before, during or after the game, according to Bailey.

"What's the occasion?" Jamie asked.

Kendry let go of the steering wheel with one hand and ran her hand down her thigh. "I don't think wearing jeans calls for an occasion."

Jamie raised his gaze from her boots to her face and quirked one eyebrow. "I meant, what's the occasion, because you are choosing to drive. Are those new jeans? They look good."

Kendry put her hand back on the wheel. "You could sit in the back with Sam, if you wanted to."

"Wow. What did you do to your hair?" Jamie ducked his head a bit to look into the cab.

"I got it cut."

"It's…really different."

Some feminine part of Kendry felt put out. Just a tiny bit. Couldn't he say something besides *it's different?* It was bad enough he'd thought her choice to drive was more noticeable than her new outfit.

Jamie rounded the hood of the truck and jumped in the front seat, but he kept staring at her.

"It's not that different," she said, putting the truck in gear.

"It's nice. Really nice."

Jamie rested his arm across the back of the bench seat, and she felt him finger a curl near her shoulder. The sensation of being touched in such a personal way crossed the line from friendly to intimate. Maybe nice wasn't so boring. If he felt the desire to touch her hair, then Kendry could love nice.

Jamie gave her hair a slight tug. "I bet Sam has been yanking on this all day."

Lesson learned. She was Sam's mother in Jamie's eyes. They were pals. Co-parents. If she'd expected a new hairstyle to be a turning point in that relationship, then she wasn't keeping real life separate from her fantasies.

"It gives him something to grab besides my glasses," she said. Out of the corner of her eye, she saw Jamie smile at her dry joke.

She took a deep breath before her next rehearsed line, inhaling the traces of Jamie's woodsy aftershave, enjoying it more than ever, now that it didn't make her sneeze. It smelled masculine and inviting. "I want to take you somewhere special to eat."

Lord, that had come out all wrong. Too husky. Too serious. She changed her tone to flippant. "Ask me what's for dinner."

"What's for dinner?" They'd come to a red light. Jamie let go of her hair and turned around to interest Sam in a toy.

"Stadium nachos."

He stopped jiggling the toy. "Nachos?"

"Doesn't that sound delicious?"

"That sounds hard to swallow."

"For a baby? Yes, which is why I already fed Sam. Quinn told me you graduated from Sam Houston High, so I looked them up. They've got a home game tonight, and I thought this would give you a chance to go somewhere besides the hospital and the house."

"My work schedule keeps me away from Sam too much as is."

"Well, you'll notice he's coming with us."

Oops. That had sounded a little more irritated than cute, but she'd been anxious with the light turning yellow as she'd entered the intersection. She came to a halt at the next light, stopping a full length behind the car in front of her, and tried again. "You must like football. We have that picture of you volunteering to be the doctor for a team."

"That was before Afghanistan. I had more time then. I couldn't begin to volunteer for the football team now."

"You don't have to. You were going to make time to eat dinner tonight, right? I'm just asking you to eat dinner at the stadium."

Friday night rush-hour traffic was taking all of Kendry's concentration. She couldn't recall her carefully persuasive phrases and the gentle arguments she'd lined up.

"I thought you understood," Jamie said. "With Sam's medical concerns, he's my only after-work concern."

A driver cut in front of Kendry, and she tapped the brakes a little too hard, angry at the stranger's carelessness. "Sam isn't sick," she bit out through clenched teeth.

"I can't believe you said that." Jamie sounded stunned. "Are we talking about the same kid? He was born prematurely, with a bad heart and poor swallowing reflexes. We have to track his development. He's—"

"He's not sick. He's got a couple birth defects that are being fixed, but in the meantime, he's not sick."

"We dodged that pneumonia bullet. We were lucky."

"Yes, we were, but you know what else, Jamie? His immune system overcame that challenge. He's not an invalid. He's actually pretty normal, and he and I want to *do* something normal tonight. We want to go to a football game at his dad's old high school."

Jamie was silent. Kendry couldn't take her eyes off the road to gauge his facial expression. One second of inattention was all it took for an accident to happen and a life to be altered.

"I don't think of Sam as an invalid," Jamie said. "I just don't think a football game is a great place for a baby."

"I brought him a bottle and some cookies. If he gets fussy, we can leave, okay? But I think Sam is going to love his first real live football game."

Right on cue, like a little gift from heaven, Sam squealed in happy agreement.

When the silence continued, she added softly, "Maybe I'm the one who needs to see something besides the hospital and the house."

Jamie only grunted. Kendry finally stole a peek at his profile. He didn't look angry, just resigned.

"Was that grunt a manly sound of agreement?" she asked, trying to lighten the mood.

Jamie sighed dramatically and leaned against the headrest. "That," he said, gazing at the roof above him, "is the sound of a man who has lost his first argument with his wife."

Kendry welcomed the little bubble of happiness in her chest. "Was it so bad?"

Jamie rolled his head from left to right. "That depends."

"On what?"

"On whether or not the Sam Houston Huskies win tonight. I'd hate to go through one humiliating defeat only to watch another."

The little happiness bubbles multiplied. "In that case," she said, joining the long line into the stadium parking lot, "go team, go."

Jamie had never seen Kendry so excited. He had to admit, the bright stadium lights against the night sky stirred a certain something in the soul. The sound of the marching band warming up under the bleachers and the smell of the gooey, artificially orange cheese substance on the corn chips were a combination he hadn't realized he'd forgotten.

Kendry was loving it. It was obvious in the bounce in her

step and the smile on her face. "Isn't this great?" she kept asking. "It's so All-American, you know?"

Jamie was reminded how different his upbringing had been from Kendry's. He hadn't missed a home game in four years of high school. Kendry hadn't made a complete semester in America. She carried Sam and the nachos as she led the way from the snack bar to the bleachers. Jamie followed with the empty car seat and the drinks, wondering how the scene looked through her eyes.

He'd never considered all that Kendry had missed because of her unconventional upbringing. Not being part of a sports team, for example. He looked at her speculatively as she led the way up the bleachers' metal stairs. What sport would she have played, if she'd had the chance? He had no idea what she enjoyed. With her slender build, she looked like she'd run cross-country, maybe. She wasn't too tall, but in those jeans, it was easy to tell that she was all legs.

At that moment, Kendry looked over her shoulder at him, an automatic move to see if he was still following. He was, and damn if he didn't feel like he'd been caught checking her out. His own wife. As if a man would check out his own—

Well, yes, he supposed most men did check out their own wives. That's how women became wives in the first place, wasn't it?

That wasn't how Kendry had become his wife. It seemed wrong to start checking her out now, not when they'd made promises to each other for a different kind of relationship. Theirs had been entered into from a logical standpoint, knowing they would be compatible, having similar values toward family and shared interests in things like medicine.

It was the kind of relationship a woman might hope for if she lived in a country like Afghanistan. The kind of relationship a woman in that part of the world would trust her family to contract on her behalf. The kind of relationship Amina had probably grown up dreaming about.

Jamie had given Amina's dream to Kendry.

He stumbled on the next step and caught himself, looking down at his own jeans and well-worn boots. He was a born and raised Texan, as Western as a man could be. Kendry, in her red sweater and blue jeans, looked as American as a slice of apple pie in a suburban high school stadium.

Neither one of them was from Amina's world, yet he expected his American bride to keep to an Afghani-style commitment to family, not to romance. Slowly climbing the stairs with a hundred other people, listening to the marching band playing a fight song as the announcer directed his attention to the home team running onto the field, Jamie felt like he was in the right place for the wrong reasons.

Yes, he should be at his alma mater's game with his wife and his child. But should he be in a relationship where admiring the way his wife sashayed up a set of bleachers was off-limits?

That's what you offered. That's what she accepted. You can't change the rules now. You'll embarrass her by checking her out.

But Jamie couldn't keep his eyes off her now. It was like being told not to think about a pink elephant. He was trying not to think about his wife's body, trying not to look at the swish of her hair, trying not to admire the glimpses of her face as she searched the rows for available seats.

She turned to talk to him again, making Jamie feel like he'd been caught with his hand in the cookie jar. Jeez, this was ridiculous.

"Is this high enough, do you think?" she asked, beaming with excitement. "I want to see everything."

A man's voice, unexpected but instantly recognizable, called out behind him. "Jamie MacDowell. Heard you were back from overseas. Good to see you."

"Luke." Jamie greeted his old football teammate, someone he'd once spent four hours a day with, five days a week, during Austin autumns like this one. "Good to see you, too."

He meant it. It had been two years since Jamie had left for Afghanistan, but Luke was looking good as always, still physically fit, unlike too many of their friends who'd become desk jockeys at office jobs. They shook hands.

"You've been a stranger."

"Just busy," Jamie said, an automatic excuse to answer the unspoken question. He and Luke and the rest of the crowd all moved up another step.

Jamie couldn't ignore his wife and baby standing a few steps above him. Introductions had to be made. Ready or not, Jamie was about to drop some big news on his old world. "I'd like you to meet my wife, Kendry."

"Your wife?" Luke looked shocked, the same reaction the hospital staff gave. Luke's gaze zeroed in on Sam. "You've got a baby, too?"

"Told you I've been busy. Kendry, this is Luke Waterson. We went to school together."

"How do you do, ma'am?" Luke whipped out his Sunday manners and greeted Kendry with a proper Texas twang to his tone.

Jamie knew what was coming next. He and Kendry had been through it often enough with coworkers. People would look at Sam, then at Jamie, and they'd nod to themselves, as if they understood his marriage. *Oh, he needed someone to help him take care of the baby.* Jamie didn't want to go through it. Not here. Not now. Not again.

Instead, Luke asked something no one at the hospital ever did. "How did you two meet?"

Kendry hiked Sam an inch higher on her hip. In the split second before she answered, Jamie had the horrible intuition that she was going to tell the truth, that Jamie had sought her out because he needed a mother for Sam.

Jamie didn't want the truth. He didn't want anyone to

know that his marriage was different than everyone else's. He was essentially a widower, unlike any of his friends. He had a baby who could be deported, a situation none of his friends could imagine. His marriage might be right for him, but tonight it seemed out of place, wrong for this setting and this part of his life.

"We met at the hospital," Kendry said, smiling at Luke like she was enjoying herself. "We both work there."

God, that sounded so blissfully normal, Jamie could have kissed her in relief.

"I'll bet he didn't give you a chance to say no once he'd set eyes on you."

Kendry shook her head immediately, dismissing the compliment. She was so easily flustered by compliments.

Luke must have caught her embarrassment, and being the stand-up guy Jamie would never admit out loud that he was, Luke changed the subject slightly. "I know you're not from around here, because I would have scooped you up first. How long have you been in Austin?"

As Kendry answered, Luke listened with real interest. For once, Jamie's wife was getting all the attention, not his son. He felt something fill his chest, something dangerously close to pride. Luke Waterson, one of his oldest friends, was clearly seeing what Jamie had always seen. Kendry was interesting to talk to, world-traveled and an intelligent woman. It was good to have someone else appreciate his wife.

Luke turned to him. "You kept her out of my sight until you got a ring on her finger. Smart man. You know I've always had a soft spot for redheads."

A redhead? Jamie looked up at her again. Sure enough, lit by the stadium lights from above, his wife was a dazzling full-color woman against the black night sky behind her. Her hair shone more red than brown, thick and wavy.

Sexy as hell.

Back in the day, he and Luke would have fallen all over themselves trying to catch the attention of a woman like this.

Kendry laughed at something Luke said, and her smile lit her green eyes. Although she held a baby, men were still taking a second glance as they passed her on the bleacher stairs.

She looked as sexy as hell, and damn if that didn't make Jamie as uncomfortable as hell. He tore his gaze away and nodded at the parents around them. "We better take a seat before kickoff, or all this Texas friendliness will disappear real quick."

"Football is serious around here," Luke said to Kendry. "No one knows that better than 'The Doctor.'" He clapped Jamie on the shoulder. "Hey, you really are a doctor now, aren't you? That there's what you'd call ironic."

"Clever as always, Waterson. You sitting with us?"

"Can't. Got a date. High maintenance, and I expect it's already gonna cost me dearly for making her sit alone this long." He nodded at Kendry again. "Good to meet you. *Great* to meet you." To Jamie, he said, "You know I'm going to hound you for more details. Jamie MacDowell is a married man, and my momma is gonna want to know everything. You know how it works."

"I know how it works." Jamie's arrival at the stadium with a woman and a baby was going to top everyone's list tomorrow morning when they recapped the game with family and friends. Unless, perhaps, the team did something astounding on the field.

Go team, go.

Chapter Nineteen

"Luke seemed really nice."

His wife spoke conversationally while they completed a complex exchange of items that ended with Sam in Jamie's lap, nachos in Kendry's lap, a car seat on the bench below them, a diaper bag in the car seat and two cups of icy soda set carefully under the metal bench they sat on.

"What did he mean when he said it was ironic that you were a doctor?" she asked.

Sam lunged for the nachos, so Jamie dug around in the diaper bag for Sam's cookies. "It was a nickname I had in school. The Doctor."

"Because your dad was a doctor?"

"It started sophomore year. I was the backup quarterback and got called in for the fourth quarter. We won." He shrugged. "Coach said the team was dying, and I'd brought them back to life. The Doctor. Maybe it did have something to do with my dad."

"Stop." Kendry looked like she was in shock. "Stop."

"What?"

"Are you telling me you were the high school quarterback?"

"I wasn't the starter until junior year, but yeah."

"I married the high school quarterback? Are you kidding me?"

Jamie couldn't tell if this was a bad thing or a good thing. Kendry was absolutely wide-eyed. She'd grabbed his arm in her intensity.

"Is this significant somehow?" he asked. "We're talking about twelve years ago."

Kendry threw back her head and laughed. "Oh, my gosh. My mom is going to flip out. I'm about to flip out. Me, little old me, married to the high school quarterback."

Jamie watched her laugh and listened to her go on for a moment. Who knew that Kendry had a thing for quarterbacks? He shook his head and spoke to Sam. "She's gone off the deep end, son."

"You don't understand. My mom hated the cold weather. I spent every fall and winter taking correspondence courses under coconut trees on whatever island called to my parents that year. But deep down, my dearest secret wish was to cheer on guys in shoulder pads.

"When I did go to high school, it was a tiny place that had kindergarten through twelfth grade in one building. Still, even at that little country school, even in the spring when the season was over, the quarterback was the Big Man on Campus. I didn't stand a chance with him. But you," she said, gesturing from his chest to the stadium at large, "at this practically NFL stadium, you were the quarterback of a real team. And I married *you*." Kendry nearly squealed the last word and thumped his arm for good measure.

"You're telling me I can still get mileage with girls for being a high school has-been quarterback?"

"I'm your wife. I'm the one who gets mileage for snagging the quarterback." Kendry popped a chip in her mouth and winked at him.

Winked at him? Serious Kendry, so interested in kidney-function tests and lumbar punctures?

Jamie wasn't certain he could resist this new version. Sexy hair, tight jeans, flirting and laughing. The desire to sleep with her had never been stronger.

The familiar guilt returned. Lust wasn't the same thing as love. Amina should be the one sitting next to him in the bleachers. Amina should be handing a cookie to Sam.

Amina hadn't wanted this life.

Jamie looked around the stadium. The Huskies were winning. The band was in full regalia, filing out of the stands and lining up behind the end zone, preparing for the half-time show. Parents and fans filled the stands, cheered their boys, called greetings to each other.

Kendry scooted an inch closer to him on the metal bench. She still held his arm, and squeezed it in excitement. "Look how big the marching band is. This is like something out of a movie. I love your school."

Kendry thought his life was wonderful. Everything Amina had rejected, Kendry wanted.

What he had was good. It really was. Amina hadn't been the right woman for his life.

And that thought, that one unacceptably disloyal thought, was enough to kill his joy in the evening. What was wrong with him? He'd loved Amina. They'd created a child together—something else it was disloyal to doubt—and he couldn't blame her for not wanting to leave her mission and her world. If she hadn't died in childbirth, they would have worked things out, somehow. They hadn't been able to find a way during the eight months before Sam was born, but they would have come to some compromise, had she lived.

The woman sitting next to him now hadn't asked for any

compromise. Kendry had agreed to live with him on his terms, wholly.

He looked down to see Kendry's hand, plain and unadorned, touching his thigh to get his attention. Amina had refused to wear an engagement ring for fear of alienating the local women she wanted to help. Rings symbolized romance. Amina found that immodest. Kendry had married him without one.

"Are you okay?"

"Fine." He looked into her eyes, sometimes hazel, sometimes green, but always pretty and full of true concern. "Thanks for asking."

Thank you for wanting what I have to offer.

He leaned over and kissed her cheek. Gently, gratefully, unrushed. He lingered for a moment, feeling the softness of her skin under his lips, the brush of her hair on his face.

He wasn't breaking any rules. As he'd told her, he couldn't love her like he'd loved Amina. But that didn't mean he couldn't value the tenderhearted woman he'd made his wife.

Kendry leaned forward to fuss with the diaper bag, breaking their contact. Her hair hid her face as she pulled out a blanket for Sam.

Sam was the reason he'd made this woman his wife. For a minute, Jamie had forgotten that this was all about Sam. It had almost felt like it was all about his marriage.

"We can go now, if you're tired," Kendry said. "It's getting colder."

"Sam's happy where he is. Let's stay. You want to see the halftime show pretty badly, I'll bet, even if the quarterback doesn't do a thing in it."

Her grin bloomed into a full smile under the white lights. "How'd you know? I hope they have baton twirlers and flag wavers and all that stuff."

"They do. You are about to see a true-blue, all-American halftime show, Mrs. MacDowell. Enjoy."

He gave her bare hand a squeeze.

I'm going to buy her a wedding ring.

It didn't mean his heart wasn't still with Amina, but he shared a life now with Kendry. For better or worse, he and Sam were living an American life, and this Mrs. MacDowell, the one he'd actually married instead of the one he'd planned to marry, should have a wedding ring.

The morning after the football game, Kendry and Sammy waited by the front door in their pajamas before Jamie left once more for a weekend of army reserve duty.

"It's only one night this time," Jamie said. "The time will fly."

Kendry smiled at his words, so similar to what he'd said in September. She'd wondered then if he were trying to convince her or himself. She knew him better now; he was trying to convince himself that he wouldn't be gone long.

"Hardly more than a long day at work," Kendry said, trying to keep her voice upbeat as her two guys hugged. Her heart broke a little as Jamie pressed his forehead to his son's for a long moment. They were so different, a large man and a petite baby, but they so clearly belonged together.

Kendry was certain the main reason Jamie had married her, the reason she could call these two guys her own, was to care for Sam if Jamie got called to active duty and sent back to war indefinitely. She prayed she'd never see these two part for more than a weekend's drill.

"Okay, buddy. Time for you to go with Mommy."

At the word *Mommy,* Sammy turned toward Kendry and pointed.

Kendry's breath caught. She felt electric, like she was watching a winning touchdown.

"Mmah," Sammy said, savoring the long *m.*

"That's right," Jamie said, sounding as excited as Kendry felt. "That's Mommy."

"Mmah." Sammy dove toward Kendry with all the justified confidence of one who knew he'd be caught.

"Oh," Kendry said, kissing his cheek as she settled him on her hip. "Just…oh." She felt tears well up.

"I think he said '*Mom*,' don't you?" Jamie smoothed his hand over Sammy's back.

"Yes!" Kendry laughed at the squeak in her own voice.

As he had the last time he left them, Jamie let his hand drift from Sam to her chin. His fingertips didn't slide down to her shoulder and away. This time, he brushed her hair away from her cheek, burying his hand in the tumble of her hair, cupping the back of her head gently.

He's going to kiss me.

She didn't move. Didn't breathe. But her heart pounded, and she felt everything vividly. The warmth of his hand, the weight of Sam in her arms, the brush of Jamie's camouflage pants against her pajama bottoms.

The heat of his lips, surprisingly soft, achingly gentle against her own, for one brief, perfect moment.

Then he was stepping back, picking up his heavy duffel bag, and not quite making eye contact with her as he opened the front door.

"You two have a good weekend."

"Be safe," Kendry said. "Come home tomorrow."

"You couldn't keep me away." With a wink, he headed for his truck.

The way he said it jogged her memory. Only two months ago, when Jamie had come to the playroom to pick up Sam after work, he'd told Kendry that he'd be back tomorrow, that she couldn't keep him away. Bailey had been certain—for about five minutes—that Jamie was interested in Kendry.

Kendry had wished it were true.

Maybe it was safe now to wish for more. She hoped so, because she couldn't stop herself from wanting to be so much more than her husband's friend.

Chapter Twenty

Jamie came home hours earlier than Kendry had expected, but she'd been ready. She'd washed her hair, then blown it dry in its beach waves, and then fretted that it looked too obvious that she'd done her hair. She wore a cheerful yellow sweater over her jeans and boots, then worried that the boots gave away how deliberately she'd chosen her outfit, so went barefoot. She cleaned her glasses. She put on lip gloss, then decided the lip gloss was too much for a woman who was supposed to be hanging out in her own house on a Sunday.

It was all in vain, because the man who came home was not the same man who'd kissed her before he left.

Jamie said hello, as if he'd just returned from a day at the hospital instead of a weekend in the army. He didn't ask where Sam was, although Kendry supposed it was obvious that he was still napping.

"How was your weekend? Was it full of exciting, top-secret army stuff?" The drill weekends were routinely dull, according to Jamie, but she wanted to cajole him into talking.

Jamie flipped through Saturday's mail, which she'd carefully piled on its usual corner of the kitchen counter. He pushed aside the top pieces, looked at the bottom pieces, and then…stood there.

Something was definitely wrong.

Kendry tried to smile naturally. "Did you notice the college catalogs? Every nursing program in the city sent me their materials. It's going to be exciting to read through it all."

Jamie looked at her briefly, and a ghost of a smile passed over his mouth. "That's good."

Then he reached into the cargo pocket on his camouflage pants and pulled out a handful of tattered white business envelopes. He added them to the pile.

"We had mail call this morning. Things sent to my last unit finally caught up to me."

The addresses were lines of letters and numbers, with forwarding stamps and more handwritten numbers. No wonder they had taken months to catch up to him. They looked official, because they had the kind of government seals in the upper left corner that her mail from the court usually bore.

Then he pulled out a padded manila envelope. The square outline of a DVD case had rubbed through the worn surface.

Kendry bit her unglossed lip. Jamie's face was expressionless, unnaturally so. She wanted to touch him. She reached a hand out and tapped the padded envelope instead, taking in the return address at a glance. "Who do you know in London?"

"It's not really from London. It's from Afghanistan." He held the padded manila envelope a moment longer, then put it down. "Do you think Sam will sleep much longer?"

"Yes. He went down about twenty minutes ago."

Jamie rubbed the back of his neck. "I need to watch this

DVD and get it over with. I'll shower while I charge my laptop and…" His words drifted off.

Kendry had never seen him so unfocused, so distracted. "I'll watch it in my bedroom."

Kendry made one last, lame attempt at a joke. "So it's actually top secret, then?"

Jamie grabbed the envelope in a decisive motion, his face as grim as if he were being forced to declare a patient dead. "It's about to be shown all over the world, actually. It's the documentary they were filming the day Amina died."

Sam's second surgery was scheduled toward the end of the week. Kendry knew it would be more involved than the heart patch. Repairing a cleft palate required scalpels and stitching, and the recovery was going to be painful for her child. The surgery itself was scheduled to take longer than the heart procedure, too. This gave Kendry time to sit next to the silent man whose name she shared, the man who hadn't smiled in days.

Sam had been understandably fussy as they waited for his surgery, since no eleven-month-old child could understand why he had to be fasting. Despite the demands of keeping Sammy as calm as she could, Kendry had noticed Jamie's peculiar tension. He'd hedged his answers to the hospital registration clerk, providing the same written statement that he'd attempted to get a replacement copy of Sam's birth documents from the embassy in Kabul. Attempted, but not yet succeeded.

Without the embassy's report of birth, Sam still had no Social Security number. So far, Jamie's health insurance had been covering Sam as his dependent, but for this surgery, the clerk had asked Jamie to sign an affidavit that he'd pay all expenses in the event that coverage was denied.

In the surgical waiting room, Kendry and Jamie settled into side-by-side chairs, which lasted about two minutes.

Jamie stood. He paced. He walked over to the coffeepot, then walked back again without pouring a cup. He sat. Just as Kendry put her hand on his shoulder, he stood and started the whole process over again.

She was ready for him when he returned to the chair. She waved the paging device in her hand. "Let's go for a walk. They'll let us know when he's in recovery."

"No, thanks."

A piece of the old Kendry, the dutiful orderly, wanted to sit silently and be a good, obedient girl. But another piece, a stronger piece, felt she had the right to make this decision for the two of them.

Maybe because she was worried about her child, or maybe because she'd been referred to as "Mrs. MacDowell" all morning, or maybe because she knew that whatever was wrong had everything to do with Jamie's military mail call and nothing to do with her, Kendry stood and reached for Jamie's hand, tugging him with her. "Let's walk."

Kendry kept up the small talk as they made their way to the park in the center of the complex. "That room was too small for you to pace in. Besides, you were scaring the other families. You were scaring me, and I know this is a minor operation, not a heart transplant."

He gave her hand a quick squeeze in agreement.

Kendry slowed their pace once they were outdoors. The October days had been quite warm, but this close to dawn, at the early hour surgeons seemed to prefer to work, there was a definite chill in the air.

She and Jamie probably looked like a contented couple, he in his leather jacket and she in the red peacoat she'd purchased as a fall-to-winter staple. They stayed on the meandering path that led past the glorious autumn colors of a large sumac tree as Kendry headed for the most private bench in the park, the one she'd thought would hide her when the cost of her pink scrubs had derailed all her careful plans.

She didn't care about those plans anymore. Those meager hopes and dreams no longer existed. She wasn't Kendry Harrison, a solo woman focusing on a sole career goal. She was Kendry MacDowell, in a nontraditional marriage that still formed the basis of a traditional family.

She dreaded the conversation she was going to have with Jamie when they reached the bench, but this was her family and her life. She needed to know what was going on, for better or worse.

"I don't think you're mourning Amina."

Kendry's voice was soft but firm, familiar to Jamie in a way that soothed. It took a moment for the actual words to sink in. Not so soothing. Jamie's first response was surprise at the sudden topic. His second was to be offended. "Of course I'm mourning Amina. I will always mourn her."

With that knee-jerk declaration out of the way, Jamie had nothing else to say. The two of them never discussed Amina. They discussed Sam and their work at the hospital. They talked about nursing schools. Lately, they'd mentioned getting a dog, but they never spoke about Amina.

Jamie changed their grip, threading his fingers between Kendry's. He wasn't ready for this. He'd never be ready for this.

Kendry apparently was. "I thought seeing that DVD must have refreshed all your memories of Amina. I was hoping it would be at least bittersweet for you."

Kendry would hope such a thing. What other woman would hope he'd remember good things about a former love?

Not former. Forever. He still loved Amina. He did.

"You've been so withdrawn, though, that I assumed seeing that DVD must have intensified your grief instead. I tried to put myself in your shoes. If I'd loved someone like you loved Amina, what would I do when his memory became painful?"

It was a rhetorical question. He wasn't expected to fill the silence that came after. Thank God.

They sat on the bench. She angled her whole body toward him, her knee brushing his thigh, their hands interlinked. "If I were missing someone, I would have clung to the baby we created together. I would have taken comfort in the miracle my lover left behind."

The miracle my lover left behind. That was Sam. Jamie wanted to tell Kendry she'd gotten it exactly right. He wanted to thank her for putting it into words for him.

If he spoke, he might choke on this sudden emotion. He couldn't speak.

Kendry could, and she did. Deliberately, carefully, logically. "But you've been very distant from Sam this week. You look at him with such longing, Jamie, but you don't hold him every second that you can, not anymore. It's like there's a pane of glass between you, and you are looking at something in a store window that you want, but you can't have."

It was frightening to have someone see him so clearly. Frightening to know he could no longer hide.

It was time to tell Kendry, whether he was ready or not.

Chapter Twenty-One

Kendry sat on the bench, studying Jamie's face while he studied their hands. She heard the siren of an approaching ambulance carry over the hospital walls.

"I don't know how to have this conversation," Jamie said. He let go of her hand and stood up, shoving his hands in his jacket's pockets. "There's a dinner event here in Austin, soon. A fund-raiser that goes with the documentary. We'll all be seeing it on the big screen. If that mail had taken much longer to catch up with me, we'd have missed it."

"We can still miss it. You aren't required to relive anything in a movie theater." Kendry didn't want to see it herself. She didn't want to know Amina better. As a vague, faceless ghost, she was already too much competition. "We can pack the DVD away for Sam. Someday, he will treasure that film of his mother."

Jamie kicked a few tree leaves off the sidewalk with the toe of his plain, black boot. "I have to be there. I owe them."

"You owe whom, what?"

"They were filming forty miles away when Amina went into labor. That may not sound like a great distance, but over there, it can be days of trekking on foot. The crew gave a ride to the midwife who was left with Sam. She never would have made it to the base before Sam died of dehydration, otherwise. The cameraman and the producer stayed. They wrote letters attesting to the fact that I was the father of Amina's baby."

"Is that some kind of Afghani tradition?"

"It's an American legal requirement. If I can provide proof of paternity to the embassy, then Sam's a U.S. citizen."

Kendry remembered those other redirected envelopes, the ones with the official seals. At this morning's patient registration, Jamie had denied that he'd gotten a reply from the embassy.

Maybe he hadn't. "When do you have to give this proof to the embassy?"

"I did, when Sam was born. Actually, a whole group of us did. At our base, there was no way to feed Sam. No formula. No wet nurses among the locals. We kept Sam on IVs, but time was running out. Guys in my unit spent their internet minutes to read State Department regulations instead of emailing their families. Everyone helped put together a packet with the witness letters and my statement. We did a quick blood-type test. Then Sam and I got out on the next plane to a U.S. base in Germany. I had to trust the film crew to deliver the packet to the embassy in Kabul. It's not the kind of thing you can drop in the mail." He reached up and yanked a leaf off the tree. "There is no mail in Afghanistan."

"Is that the problem? They didn't deliver the packet?"

"They did. Amina was their friend, and they knew her baby had no chance as an orphan in Afghanistan. There is no adoption in that country. Officially, there are no orphanages."

Jamie dropped the leaf, then reached up and yanked another one off.

Kendry stood and took the leaf out of his hand. "What is on that DVD that has to do with this paternity paperwork?"

"Another man." She watched Jamie force the words through a tight throat and clenched jaw. "There was another man."

"Another man who did what?" The obvious answer came to her before Jamie could form a reply. Kendry's world tilted. She grabbed Jamie's arm. "But Sam is yours. There were blood tests."

Jamie steadied her with a strong hand on her other arm. "Blood tests can rule out paternity, but they don't prove it. Our blood types only mean it's possible that I'm the father."

Numbly, she sank to the bench with Jamie.

"I'm sorry," he said, rubbing her arms briskly. "I don't know how to make this less of a shock for you."

Anger exploded inside her. How dare Amina deceive Jamie? How dare this woman lie to Jamie about carrying another man's child?

"Oh, Jamie," Kendry managed to choke out, despite the fury clogging her throat. "That DVD must have been devastating."

Her husband had fought so long and so hard for his son, only to learn this week that Sam's mother might have been unfaithful to him. Kendry wanted to defend Jamie, but against what? A dead woman's betrayal? She couldn't fix that. Tears of helplessness stung her eyes. She cupped Jamie's face in her hands, his strong jaw warm in her palms. "I'm so sorry."

"No, it wasn't like that." Jamie took her hands and held them close to his chest, inside his open jacket. "I'm not explaining this right."

Although Kendry was practically vibrating with outrage,

she could feel Jamie's heartbeat through his shirt. Steady, strong—this wasn't a shock to him.

"I've always known there was someone before I met Amina, another soldier who was killed in action. She didn't cheat on me the way you're thinking."

Kendry drew in a shaky breath. "Then what does this other man have to do with Sam?"

Jamie's voice remained steady, that of a man who gave commands during crisis, but the anguish in his eyes was unmistakable. "Haven't you noticed, Kendry? Sam looks nothing like me."

"He must look like Amina."

"He's supposed to be premature, but he's hitting all his milestones on time. I had no doubts, none whatsoever, throughout the pregnancy. None during those first six months in Germany. But lately, the possibility that Amina was already pregnant when I met her has been getting harder and harder to ignore."

"You said there was no adoption in Afghanistan. Even if Sam isn't biologically yours, you would never send him back there."

Jamie pressed his hand over hers, keeping it near his heart. "I've got a lawyer who specializes in immigration, but we're in uncharted territory. There's never been a case like this. I was supposed to bring that packet to the embassy in person, for example. We had to get a judge to rule for an exception on that. I've got to make that original packet suffice. Anything to prevent a DNA test, in case my suspicion is right. I can't let Sam be deported to Afghanistan."

Deflated from the rush of anger that apparently hadn't been called for, Kendry pulled her hands back and leaned forward, resting her arms on her knees, letting her hair hide her face. "When were you going to tell me all this?"

"Never." The wooden bench shifted as Jamie stood again, ready to take action, although there was none to take. "The embassy would acknowledge Sam's birth, and I'd never tell you there was a chance Sam wasn't really mine."

Another leaf was plucked, crumpled, tossed. "Sam is mine. He is, damn it, in every way that counts."

Kendry shut her eyes at the fierce pain in his voice. Losing Sam would devastate her, but she was afraid it would destroy Jamie. Afraid, because anything that caused Jamie pain would hurt her, too.

She loved him. He'd married her for horribly practical reasons, but she'd married him because she loved him.

So she lifted her head and shook her hair back. "What can I do to help, Jamie?"

His hand froze in midair. The leaf he'd been reaching for dangled, brilliant orange, on its branch, and then Jamie was down on one knee before her, so close the she had to widen her knees to give his body room.

"How can you help?" he repeated, as if he hadn't heard her right. His hands were in her hair as he lifted her face and kissed her forehead, her cheek and then, a pause. He kissed her other cheek. "I don't deserve you, Kendry. My God, you should be furious with me."

"For what?" If her voice shook, it was because she had so much Jamie, so close. He was big, vital, startling her with his hands in her hair and his kisses on her face.

"I asked you to help me care for Sam. I told you it wouldn't be easy, but I didn't tell you every possibility."

"Jamie." She smoothed back a piece of his hair, something she'd only done once before, on the concrete floor of a garage. "No one knows every possibility when they get married. I promised 'for better or worse,' and that's that."

Jamie's eyes lowered as he focused on her mouth.

He's going to kiss me.

But he didn't. He closed his eyes briefly, then took her hands in his as he settled back on his haunches. With their hands clasped and their heads bowed, they might have looked to any passersby like they were praying.

He touched his forehead to their clasped hands. "We may go broke paying legal fees, even on a doctor's salary."

"Been there, done that. Could do it again." She wanted to lighten the mood, at least a little, so she sighed with deliberately theatrical loudness. "But I warn you, it sucks."

Jamie chuckled and lifted his head. "Kendry MacDowell, I love—" He stopped, but kept his half smile in place. "I love the way you make me smile."

He came to his feet, so Kendry stood, too, trying not to wish that he'd finished his sentence differently.

Jamie picked up the paging device and pulled her to his side as they headed back toward the waiting room, walking in sync.

Her husband valued her more than ever, but this wasn't what Kendry had wished for. Not at all.

Chapter Twenty-Two

Ten days later, Jamie's wait was over. He came home from just another day of work on an unremarkable November evening. He walked into the kitchen to find Kendry sitting at the table, feeding Sam his dinner. Sam now ate jars of baby food with great gusto as he recovered rapidly from his palate repair.

"You got a package from a law firm. It came by private courier." Kendry sounded breathless as she gestured with the baby spoon to a flat, plastic document case on the table.

Sam tracked the movement of the spoon with his entire body, keeping his mouth wide open, all his attention on the food that had taken a detour away from him. It was a classic, comical baby moment.

My God, they are precious. Perfect. I want this in my life.

Jamie looked at the courier case. For eleven months, during a rushed exit from Afghanistan, a frustrating series of nannies and doctors in Germany and the relatively peaceful routine of life in Texas, Jamie had worked and waited, battled and prayed, for one document to arrive from the State Department.

He picked up the plastic case. Inside, he'd find out if the embassy had demanded further proof of paternity.

I could lose it all.

He was a trained soldier, a physician who handled trauma. He didn't hesitate to break the seal and remove the papers inside, no matter how tragic the news could be. No matter how tight the knot in his gut.

"What is it? What does it say?" Kendry's attention was riveted on Jamie, the spoon in her hand frozen in midair.

Sam thunked his heels against his high chair and babbled a string of indignant consonants at the spoon. Jamie felt a smile tug at the corner of his mouth and the center of his heart. Still standing, he placed the paper he wanted Kendry to see on the table, took the spoon from her hand and fed Sam some mushy peas.

Kendry picked up the certificate, a work of art in shades of blue, which trembled in her hand. "This is it. 'Consular Report of Birth Abroad of a Citizen of the United States of America.' Jamie, you did it."

Jamie scraped peas off Sam's chin with the soft spoon and gave his son a second chance at them.

"This calls for champagne," Kendry said. "You're home free now. Passports, Social Security numbers…"

Jamie let her words rush over him in a soothing cascade.

"Isn't it icing on the cake that you got this news now? The premiere is the day after tomorrow. You'll be able to tell the film crew that their trip to Kabul was worth it. Do we have champagne in the house?"

Sam was hungry, mouth open and ready for more. He could eat so easily now, less than two weeks after the operation. The difference was astounding. Sometimes a person only realized how bad something had been once it got better.

Jamie slipped a plain business envelope from the case

into his back pocket and handed Kendry the spoon. "I'm going to get some air."

He watched Kendry's smile fade.

It's not you. You're perfect.

"I need a moment." He slapped the light switch for the outdoor lighting as he slid open the glass door and walked onto the back deck. He stood at the railing and looked over the lawn, nearly an acre that sloped gently away from the house, ending at a creek that served as the property line.

Jamie had bought this house because of the backyard. He'd thought it the ideal place to raise a boy. The creek was shallow enough to wade in, full of rocks to build dams. The lawn was sloped just enough to give a young football player some downhill speed if he tried to dodge a dad who had to run uphill to catch him.

But had Jamie stood next to the real estate agent and dreamed of playing ball with another man's son?

He took the envelope out of his pocket and set it on the deck railing. From the moment the ugly suspicion had whispered in his head, he'd told himself it didn't matter. Amina's past lover was dead and buried. Jamie had been the one to support her during the pregnancy. Someone had to raise Sam. Someone had to *love* Sam, forever, and Jamie was honored to be that man.

That damned DVD.

Jamie had known who the man was the moment the camera had shown Amina speaking to him. The documentary was careful not to show any of the women interacting with men in a manner that strict Afghanis could label as improper, but as Jamie had watched Amina speaking across the expanse of a table with a man identified as Corporal Anthony Schroeder, he'd known. There'd been something in Amina's smile, a look in her eyes that Jamie recognized, because she had loved him, also, after that corporal had died.

Jamie unfolded the report. Because of that DVD, the dead

man had a face. A name. And now, according to the private investigator Jamie had asked his lawyer to employ, Corporal Schroeder had a grave in South Carolina, two grieving parents and a sister. A family who might want their dead son's living, breathing baby.

My baby, damn it. Amina wouldn't have deceived me.

Amina might not have known. She would have only been weeks along. Maybe days. This Schroeder guy had died not knowing. His family had no idea.

Through the glass door, Jamie saw Kendry lift Sam out of his high chair and swing him high, celebrating the supposed safety of his citizenship.

Kendry had forgiven Jamie everything so far. She'd accepted all his terms and done all the compromising, but she was a woman of definite standards and proven strength. She didn't need him to build a good life for herself. He didn't think she'd stay with him if he gave their child away.

Life without Kendry?

God, no. He needed her. She was quick to forgive, eager to be happy. She was his best friend. His sanity.

Sam laughed at the woman who'd become the center of his world. Kendry, the beautiful woman with the long legs who spun in circles on his kitchen tiles, was the woman Sam had chosen. The woman Jamie was falling in love with. Hard.

Jamie was probably Sam's biological father. There was no need to ever find out for certain. No one except he knew the Schroeder family might be missing out on a grandchild. He crumpled the report in his fist and hurled it into the darkness.

Eventually, the sliding glass door slid open with barely a sound. "Is everything okay out here?"

Jamie clenched the porch rail.

"I know you're a soldier, but it is kind of chilly and you've been out here for a while." Kendry draped the blanket from his bed around his shoulders.

"Thank you," he said, the weight of her kindness heavy on his shoulders. "Where's Sam?"

"He's in his play saucer. I can see him from here." Kendry leaned her backside against the railing, facing him. "Did you lose a patient today? You're looking pretty grim."

"I had some thinking to do."

She tugged a corner of the blanket over his forearm. "I forget that every success with Sam must remind you that Amina is gone. But you've done right by her child. That will help, I think, if you give it time. You've jumped through a million hoops—or maybe you've pushed them all out of the way—and you've kept Sam safe."

"Don't make me out to be a hero. Please." He took the blanket off his shoulders and wrapped it around hers. "I'm not as good as you think I am. You're going to hate me, Kendry, but I need to get that DNA test."

"But why? You love that baby." The grief in Kendry's cry and the stricken look on her face made Jamie wrap his arms around her without thinking. As if he, the source of her pain, could also soothe it away.

He spoke into the warmth of her hair. "That DVD changed everything. I can't stop thinking that it could just as easily have been me. I could've been the one Amina loved first. I could've driven over that IED and died."

"Don't say such a thing." Kendry clutched him tightly, and he loved her all the more for hating the thought of him dead. He hated himself for what he was about to put her through.

"If I'd died, how would my family have welcomed the news that I'd left a child behind? I've been so narrow-minded, doing everything to keep Sam. It never occurred to me I might be denying another man's family the chance to know their son's child."

He was damn near close to sobbing. Damn close, but Kendry sobbed for him. He pressed his cheek against her hair.

"I have to order that DNA test. I'm so sorry, but I have to do it."

She stayed in his arms for longer than he would have expected, but finally, she stepped back. "You said you weren't the man I thought you were, but, Jamie, you are exactly that man. You have the courage to do the right thing, even if it hurts you."

He didn't deserve her. Even now, Kendry could see something worthwhile in him. "I don't know what I'd do if—"

"Don't worry about that yet. Maybe never."

Jamie let her silence him. He'd started to say he didn't know what he'd do if he lost her, but it wasn't the time to be placing more burdens on her. It was enough that she loved Sam. He had no right to expect her to love the man who was about to take a step that could cause them all unimaginable pain.

In the morning, they went together to a private lab that ran DNA tests. The lab tech casually informed them that the results could be ready in as little as twenty-four hours. They might get the news the day of the documentary's showing.

Kendry and Jamie agreed the timing was good. If Sam was not related to Jamie, they could confirm with the crew that Corporal Schroeder and Amina had been a couple. Jamie was going on a hunch, and they couldn't ask the surviving Schroeders to take a DNA test without knowing for certain.

She and Jamie agreed that if Schroeder wasn't the man, they needed to get the right name from the film crew. Everything was discussed politely and logically, calmly and rationally, from morning to evening.

By midnight, Kendry was exhausted from the strain of suppressing her emotions. She was sick with sympathy for what Jamie had to be feeling. She was scared to death that Sam would lose the only parent he'd known.

She was selfishly, oh, so selfishly, worried about herself. The reasons Jamie had married her were disappearing, one by one. Sam's health challenges were all but gone. He'd sailed through his two surgeries. He was eating and crawling now, babbling up a storm and didn't need any kind of extra therapy. The embassy had recognized Sam's citizenship. Jamie's military commitment was nearly over. They'd made it through two drill weekends, and he only had four more to go.

She'd be completely unnecessary four months from now. If this DNA test came out badly, she wouldn't even have that long before Jamie notified the family in South Carolina.

She didn't want to lose this new life she lived. She'd learned to be content with what she had, and what she had was the regard of a good man. If that man never stopped mourning his lover, then so be it. She'd thought they were moving toward something more, reading too much into each kiss, but that had been foolish of her. She had his friendship. They loved Sam. It was enough.

Sam was rustling around in his crib, so Kendry tiptoed down the dark hallway to his open door. She sucked in a whispered "oh" at the sight of Jamie's bare back, golden in the soft nightlight. He was bending over the crib, shirtless, as he'd been that first weekend. This time, she was wearing proper pink pajamas instead of Jamie's T-shirt, but he...dear God...he was still a picture of male strength.

Her eyes drank in his smooth skin, stretched over defined muscles that tapered in a delicious symmetry down to the low waistband of his loose flannel pants. Her entire body woke, responding to the sight. She felt warm, and her pajama top felt too heavy against her skin. Her own muscles felt the need to stretch and move, to wrap themselves around the male heat of Jamie.

He was humming quietly to his son as he rubbed his back. She watched them for a while, her two guys, one sleeping, one soothing. If the sight of Jamie made Kendry's mouth water and her body ache, then the sound of him humming to a baby made her heart no longer her own.

I could lose everything tomorrow. If Sam belongs to another family, then Jamie doesn't need me, not even for four more months.

Jamie straightened and turned toward her. Their eyes met immediately, as if he'd known she'd be there.

I'd be losing something before I really had it. And she really wanted it. There was no denying that.

His joined her in the hallway, shutting the bedroom door behind him. In a husky whisper, he said, "He's sleeping."

She drew in a breath, deliberately controlled, but the scent of warm, clean man undid her. She wanted to press herself against that bare chest. She wanted to be comforted, to be held. She wanted to be made love to.

"You couldn't sleep, either?" Jamie spoke quietly, standing so close that she could feel his body heat.

Kendry lifted her chin to look at him. "Too bad you can't rub my back and put me to bed, too."

She saw his eyes narrow, his gaze sharpen, studying her to see if she'd meant it the way it sounded. She didn't look away.

Jamie literally turned her away. Taking her by the shoulders, he turned her to face the wall, but he didn't let go. Instead, he brushed her hair aside, exposing her neck, and started kneading her shoulders. His strong hands made her feel weak as her muscle tightness was released with firm strokes. She touched the wall with her fingertips to steady herself.

Their bodies almost brushed as his hands slowed, pushing deeper. "Did I ever tell you what my plan was, if the embassy said no?"

Kendry couldn't form the right syllables, so she only shook her head.

"In the middle of nights like these, I would see myself grabbing Sam and running. Out of the country. I'd put my money in overseas bank accounts, something I could access from a tropical island."

His breath touched the back of her neck. "You've lived on a lot of islands. Tell me which one, Kendry. Tell me which one would be a safe home, and we'll run away."

His hands worked lower, his fingers pressing firmly into her flesh, following her spine.

She swallowed hard and whispered into the dark hallway. "You don't mean it."

"Don't I? Name your island, Kendry."

His hands reached her lower back, thumbs touching her skin under the hem of her pink pajama top.

She shivered.

"Say the name, and we'll fly out tomorrow. We'll go somewhere sunny and hide from the world." His lips brushed the back of her neck as he spoke, so lightly she might have imagined it. "We'll sleep in the shade of a coconut tree, warm on the sand of a beach."

Oh, how she wanted him. He was only toying with her, spinning a little fantasy that he thought was harmless.

"You would never really do it."

"You might be surprised at what I'd do. Why wouldn't I go to your island?" His hands slid around the bare skin of her waist to the softness of her stomach.

Enough.

She turned around to face him, making his hands stop their sensual play. She shook her hair back from her face and looked him in the eye. "You would never do it, Jamie, because the beaches on my island are too warm, and everyone there is bare. I'd be topless under that coconut tree, and you don't want that. You don't think of me that way."

She had the length of a heartbeat to see the look in his eyes turn dangerous.

"Oh, I think about it," he growled. Then his hands were in her hair, tilting her face up as his mouth came down on hers.

His body crowded hers against the wall, chest to chest, his hard hips against her soft waist. On her gasp of breath, he invaded her mouth, his tongue velvet, the slide smooth and sure and certain. When he broke off the kiss to speak against her lips, he sounded angry. "I know exactly what I think about. I've been imagining it since the first night we were married."

"Don't lie." Her thoughts were jumbled and further words wouldn't come, but she shook her head with a tiny, quick movement of denial.

Jamie moved one hand to her back, holding her close as he spoke and kissed his way down her neck. "You were lit from behind by the television." He licked her skin lightly. "Your legs were bare. You put a blanket over me."

Had she? She couldn't think straight, not in the arms of a man who so clearly desired her. She was being ravished, devoured, and she had no defense. She wanted none.

"Two months of imagination, Kendry. Two months of knowing you'd think less of me." His words were whispered, fervent, desperate. Her pajama top had a loose neckline, exposing her collarbone, and Jamie's hot mouth caressed the upper curve of her breast.

"I want you to put on those old glasses. I want your hair in a ponytail and your body hidden by scrubs. Anything to tame my imagination. The hell of it is, it won't work. I know you, Kendry. I know you, and I want you, and nothing you change on the surface of you will undo that. It's too late. I want my wife."

He bent his head lower. Through the thin cotton of her

top, she felt the heat and the moisture as he took the peak of her breast in his mouth, moving the rough cotton over her sensitive skin as he stroked the tip with his tongue.

He hadn't really asked her a question, but she answered him anyway.

"Yes."

Chapter Twenty-Three

Kendry woke to the sound of a baby crying, the same as she'd done every day for two months. This morning, however, she woke in Jamie's bed.

His empty bed. For a delicious moment, she thought Jamie had gone to get the baby, and she smiled into the pillow that smelled of his aftershave. He could bring the baby back to the bed and they could laze around, admiring the perfection of Sam's fingers and toes as he drank his bottle between adoring parents.

Not today. Jamie was gone. She had a fuzzy memory of rolling over in bed to see him standing in the darkness by his tall dresser, already wearing scrubs and fastening his watch. At the sound of her stirring, he'd come to her side and kissed her lightly. "Stay asleep," he'd whispered. "I have to go in. Gregory's swamped."

It was hardly the good-morning lovemaking she might have hoped for, but it was the reality of being married to an emergency physician.

Sam reminded her he was still stuck in his crib.

"I'm coming, my little alarm clock." Reluctantly, she left Jamie's bed.

When Kendry didn't hear from Jamie by midmorning, she knew he was probably still swamped. Last night had apparently been a doozy for the city, and the E.R. was undoubtedly still treating Friday night's patients well into Saturday morning.

Kendry put Sam in his stroller and went for a long walk, wondering how Jamie could concentrate at work. She could hardly think of anything except last night, of the exquisite thrill of being able to touch him without reserve, the nearly unbearable intimacy of him moving inside her, the incredible feeling of being kissed like every square inch of her skin was delicious.

She managed not to worry until lunch came and went. Either the E.R. was still ridiculously busy, or Jamie was waiting to hear the DNA results from the lab before calling her.

Couldn't he call just to tell me he...

He loved her? He hadn't said that last night.

That quickly, the terrible truth hit her: nothing had changed for him. Jamie didn't usually call her from work, so why should he call today? They'd been friends yesterday, and they were still friends today. Friends with benefits, now.

She hated the term. It was touted as highly civilized, a bit of harmless fun even, to have friends with benefits, but Kendry had never understood the philosophy. She wondered now if Jamie did.

Stop it. You'll make yourself crazy. He's probably reluctant to call until he's heard from the lab.

The DNA test. The possibility of losing Sam. Yes, Jamie had more to worry about than calling her to see if she'd enjoyed herself in his bed.

Sam drank his afternoon bottle lazily, taking his time and getting drowsy. Kendry made the effort to block out thoughts of lab tests and friends with benefits, so that Sam wouldn't be held by tense arms.

Then, finally, Jamie texted her.

Want to talk to you. E.R. slammed. Will call as soon as I can. No lab results yet.

She put Sam down for his nap. Kendry stood in the hallway and touched her fingertips to the wall. They had made love, hadn't they? It had been more than just sex. More than tension-relieving, stress-reducing sex between two consenting adults.

She glanced down the hall toward the bed they'd barely reached. Actually, they'd gone at each other like starving people at a feast. He was a man, one who hadn't taken a woman to bed in a year of mourning, a man whose world hung in the balance of a lab test, a man in desperate need of mindless relief.

Here Kendry had stood, female, healthy, willing. She'd dared him to imagine her undressed in the tropics.

A second, more terrible possibility arose. Instead of treating her as if nothing had changed, maybe Jamie hadn't called because he didn't know what to say to a woman he regretted sleeping with.

They'd mindlessly crossed a line he'd never meant to cross. He'd never wanted them to be lovers. He'd never wanted there to be "that kind of thing" between them.

Whether last night had been casual fun or a horrible mistake, one thing seemed certain: Jamie would have called if last night had made him fall in love with her.

Kendry couldn't find Jamie in the crush at the premiere. He'd sent her one more text as she was dressing for the event:

Austin gone crazy. Will have to meet you there. Quinn picking you up. No labs yet.

The hotel's conference space had been turned into a movie theater and cocktail lounge, with tables and chairs grouped before a giant screen and bartenders serving drinks from kiosks in every corner. It wasn't yet dark outside, only five o'clock in the evening, but inside, it looked like midnight.

Kendry had chosen her dress with modesty in mind, knowing many of the film crew were native Afghanis. When Kendry thought of women in Afghanistan, she pictured women who peeked suspiciously from behind scarves held over their faces.

Over Bailey's objection, Kendry had chosen a plain burgundy dress with bracelet-length sleeves and a below-the-knee hem. The round collar and the wide cuffs were trimmed in burgundy sequins, adding a subtle sparkle that saved Kendry from having to buy jewelry.

She'd guessed, correctly, that Afghani women would be present tonight, their heads covered with scarves, but they were far from plain. Colors and patterns swirled around the room, and the women looked exotic in their brilliant blues and emphatic oranges and yellows. Kendry felt dull in comparison.

At last, she saw Jamie. His back was to her, but she knew the height and breadth of him, filling out his tuxedo. She waited a step behind him as he finished his conversation, then tapped his arm.

He turned around. Not Jamie. A handsome man who smiled at her, but not Jamie.

"I'm sorry," she said. "I thought you were someone I knew."

"Who? Quinn or Jamie?" Almost immediately, as if he'd answered his own question, he called out, "Jamie."

Kendry spotted her husband cutting his way through the crowd. He wore his formal military uniform, the dark blue coat decorated with medals, the epaulettes of gold thread shining with his rank.

"Braden," Jamie said, sounding surprised as he came within a step of them. Before shaking hands or hugging his brother, Jamie stepped close enough to Kendry to kiss her cheek.

Her cheek.

Introductions followed. "I need to steal Kendry away for a moment, before the movie starts. We'll catch you at the table. Thanks for being here." They did the manly clap-on-the-shoulder thing, and then Jamie guided Kendry toward the exit with a hand on her back. "I've got news."

A man stepped into their path. "Captain MacDowell, so good to see you, sir." More men gathered around. As Jamie introduced her to the film crew, Kendry struggled to control her patience. Jamie had news, but was it good or bad?

The lights dimmed three times. The film's producer escorted them to the front of the room and sat with them at a reserved table where Braden and Quinn already waited. Another gentleman walked to a waiting microphone to address the crowd.

Kendry leaned over to Jamie. "Did you hear from the lab?" she whispered.

Jamie nodded, then stood. Surprised, Kendry looked around and realized other uniformed personnel in the audience were also standing. She felt foolish for not paying attention to the speaker.

After a round of applause, Jamie took his seat. "They won't give results over the phone. I got there just before they closed. That's why I was so late, but—"

The speaker gestured toward their table, and all eyes turned to them. Kendry, sitting between Jamie and the producer, assumed a neutral, attentive expression until the moment passed. She grabbed Jamie's leg under the tablecloth. "But?"

With his eyes on the speaker, Jamie leaned back in his chair to whisper in her ear. "Sam's mine."

Two simple words. Two incredibly important, life-altering words. Tears filled her eyes. She was happy, so happy, for Sam. He belonged with Jamie, and that was where he'd stay, loved and cherished his entire life.

The speaker finished as the movie opened with a soaring view of Afghanistan's landscape and the sounds of lush ethnic music. As the camera came in closer and closer, first to one valley, then to one village, then to one house, the music became quieter and simpler, until only one instrument was playing and one woman was laboring in a hopelessly dry garden plot.

Jamie whispered to her. "I'm sorry I put you through this. You didn't need to be dragged into it. I shouldn't have doubted her."

And then Amina filled the screen, vibrant and alive. She was young, so young, unveiled and full of energy. Long moments passed before Kendry could focus on Amina's words. They were intelligent, articulate.

Passionate.

Jamie bowed his head.

Nausea crawled up the back of Kendry's throat, fear and pain making themselves felt. This was the woman Jamie loved. How could she, plain Kendry Harrison, have ever thought to replace her?

You didn't need to be dragged into it.

Jamie would have gotten that DNA test without her. He would have survived the overnight wait without her in his bed. Perhaps he was feeling guilty for sleeping with Kendry when he loved Amina.

The film moved on, showing scenes of young girls' lives, images Kendry could hardly absorb while she studied Jamie's profile each time Amina appeared. Kendry couldn't fool herself. She was second best for Jamie. She always had been, and she always would be.

She could no longer bear to live her life that way.

When she wiped away a disobedient tear, one that refused to be blinked back, the film's producer nodded, apparently believing her tears were evoked by his people's plight.

She felt like a fake.

She had to leave. Now.

"Kendry!"

Jamie's voice cut through the night air. Kendry winced and hugged her arms more tightly around her waist. She wanted more time to brood out here alone, on the hotel's pool deck. She needed more minutes to breathe the cool November air and listen to the calming sound of the muted downtown traffic.

Jamie called her name again.

She couldn't hide from Jamie any more than she could hide from her feelings. This sparkling blue pool, brightly lit in the night but deserted at this time of year, was as good a place as any to end a marriage.

Solemnly, she stepped out from behind a concrete arch. Jamie came toward her immediately, pushing a deck chair out of his way. She nearly smiled, remembering the way he'd shoved her garage apartment's chair aside, angry when he'd thought she was a neglected child.

She wasn't neglected, and she was no child. She was done living a compromise.

"Are you all right?" The concern in his voice was genuine.

"Jamie, we need to talk." He was the kind of man who would listen. He always had been.

"Only if by *talk*, you mean this." He pulled her to him

as if she didn't have her arms wrapped protectively around her middle and kissed her without hesitation.

Her body was a traitor, responding immediately, eager for more of last night's bliss. It was so easy to give in, to let him open her mouth and taste her. Her body tried to over-rule her mind. It nearly won the battle, but as the kiss built in intensity, Kendry turned her head sharply to the side. "Stop. Please."

"Why? Why on earth—"

"I need to end this before it goes any further. For my own sake."

Jamie's breathing wasn't perfectly controlled. The hand in her hair wasn't steady. "And by *this,* what do you mean?"

She bit her lip. This was going to be hard, finishing something that she shouldn't have started. "Last night was my fault. I gave you the wrong impression."

Jamie let go of her slowly, letting his hand graze the length of her hair before he took a step back.

"I'm not a friends-with-benefits kind of girl." Now that the first words were out, the rest could follow. "I can't have sex now and then with a man I'm so in—that I'm such good friends with. It ruins our relationship."

"I won't do anything to ruin what we have. If you don't want me to touch you, then I won't touch you."

The words were meant caringly, but they also confirmed what she'd known, deep down. Sex with her was a take-it-or-leave-it situation for him. She'd been willing and avail-able, nothing more.

She uncrossed her arms and shook her hands out, cramped as they were from holding all her tension in. "I can't keep living with you."

"We've had no problems until now. I'll do whatever it takes to make you comfortable again. Our family is every-thing to me. Everything."

"You won't lose that. Sam is yours, safe and sound." She

gestured in the general direction of the ballroom. "You've got Quinn, and Braden, and your mom. Your family will always be yours."

He caught her hand and brought it to his chest. "Not my family. Our family. Our family is everything."

She felt the hard rectangles of his medals pressing into the back of her hand while he used his free hand to search his pockets.

"If you don't believe me, then believe this." He held up a band of plain gold. "I bought it for you after the football game, and I've been carrying it around ever since. I couldn't find the right time to give it to you, not after the DVD arrived. It's not the kind of thing you can give a woman while she's praying the State Department won't put up a fight."

This was too much. He was making it too hard on her. Kendry started shaking her head no, no, no.

She must have backed away because he caught her hand again, her left hand. "I couldn't give it to you while we were waiting for DNA results. Tonight isn't ideal, either, but I want you to know how serious I am about keeping us together. This is for us, you and me and Sam. Our family."

Jamie slid the ring on her finger.

Just yesterday morning, the ring would have been enough, proof that her choice to marry a friend instead of a lover was the right one. "You wouldn't risk this to sleep with me again?"

He didn't answer her. After a long moment, he dropped his gaze to her finger and rubbed his thumb over the gold band.

She placed her other hand over his. "I know I'm crazy to give you up. Having most of Jamie MacDowell is probably better than having all of someone else, but I can't do it."

"I love you, Kendry."

Her heart tripped, but the reality was that he loved her

as his friend, as family. She tried to drop her hand, but he held firm.

"I love you," he said again. "If you need to leave, then I won't stop you, but I will follow you. What I said about never touching you again was a lie. I'm going to try to touch you as often as possible, Kendry. I'm going to do everything I can to make you want me, and when you do, I'm going to make love to you until you're helpless with pleasure. Then I'm going to bring you back home and continue loving you, forever."

Her body responded with an immediate, aching desire. Her heart cried yes, but she let the first thrilling shiver pass and kept her mind clear. "I'm nothing like Amina. I'll never be like her."

"Amina?" He was taken aback, so surprised that she was able to pull her hand away. "Of course you aren't. I don't expect you to be."

She gestured again toward the ballroom. "I understand now, Jamie. I get it. She was a truly special person, one of those charismatic people that aren't afraid of anything. You'll never forget her. How could you, when you have Sam? But even if Sam didn't exist, you'd never get over her. That makes your next lover second best."

"That's not true."

"There's nothing you can do about it. She was once in a lifetime. I get that, too. But I know me, and I know my heart, and it will tear me up to stay married to you and know that I'm second best."

"Second best? Is that how you see yourself?"

She stepped closer to the pool. The light under the water reflected upward, catching the sequins of her dress in a muted way after sparkling through the water first. "I'm just me. Pretty simple. Not too interesting."

"You're amazing. Always. Every time I look at you, I see

something new. Right now, your eyes look blue. You're a brunette in this moonlight."

"I'm always a brunette."

"No, you're not. You were a redhead in the stadium. Your hair was black silk on my pillow last night."

She felt her cheeks flush.

"Do you know what color your eyes were when we met? They were hazel. When you hold my son, they're green. Do you know what I thought when I sat down across from you during that first lunch?"

She shook her head.

"I thought to myself, 'I could look at her across a kitchen table for the rest of my life.' It's not a matter of hair and eyes. They're just a reflection of you, a woman of depths and layers, a woman who fascinates me."

When she turned away in disbelief, he caught her shoulders and turned her back to face him. "It's true, Kendry. I was falling in love with you from that first day, even when I told myself it wasn't possible."

"Because you loved Amina."

"Yes. But you were Kendry, and I couldn't not love you. The more I knew you, the more I wanted to know you. You are always interesting, always surprising, but you are always, always my Kendry."

With a gentle touch, he brushed her hair behind her ear. "I'm not offering you the old love I had for someone else. What I feel for you is whole and new, a love for you. Only you."

Jamie dropped to one knee.

The night must have moved on. The city must have continued its business, but for Kendry, her entire world was the man before her.

He took another ring out of his pocket, one with diamonds that caught every glimmer of available light and then threw it back into the night tenfold.

He reached for her hand and kissed the plain gold band reverently. "I realized a wedding ring wasn't enough. It's only part of our lives. That ring says we're a family, Kendry, but this ring…" He slid the circle of faceted light onto her finger, letting it touch the gold. "This ring says I love you."

He hadn't really asked her a question, but Kendry answered him anyway, laughing through tears as joy filled her heart.

"Yes."

"Let me ask you. Kendry Ann Harrison MacDowell, will you be the love of my life?"

"Yes," she said again, so he'd stand and hold her and kiss her like a woman wanted to be kissed by the man she loved.

Jamie stood, but as she tilted her head back for his kiss, he asked her one more question. "Will you let me take you on a honeymoon? I've got a vision of you under a coconut tree that's driving me out of my mind."

"Yes," she whispered, and then he kissed her exactly as a man wildly in love with his bride should.

* * * * *

REQUEST YOUR FREE BOOKS!

2 FREE NOVELS PLUS 2 FREE GIFTS!

✦HARLEQUIN®

SPECIAL EDITION

Life, Love & Family

YES! Please send me 2 FREE Harlequin® Special Edition novels and my 2 FREE gifts (gifts are worth about $10). After receiving them, if I don't wish to receive any more books, I can return the shipping statement marked "cancel." If I don't cancel, I will receive 6 brand-new novels every month and be billed just $4.74 per book in the U.S. or $5.24 per book in Canada. That's a savings of at least 14% off the cover price! It's quite a bargain! Shipping and handling is just 50¢ per book in the U.S. and 75¢ per book in Canada.* I understand that accepting the 2 free books and gifts places me under no obligation to buy anything. I can always return a shipment and cancel at any time. Even if I never buy another book, the two free books and gifts are mine to keep forever.

235/335 HDN F45Y

Name	(PLEASE PRINT)

Address		Apt. #

City	State/Prov.	Zip/Postal Code

Signature (if under 18, a parent or guardian must sign)

Mail to the Harlequin® Reader Service:
IN U.S.A.: P.O. Box 1867, Buffalo, NY 14240-1867
IN CANADA: P.O. Box 609, Fort Erie, Ontario L2A 5X3

Want to try two free books from another line?
Call 1-800-873-8635 or visit www.ReaderService.com.

* Terms and prices subject to change without notice. Prices do not include applicable taxes. Sales tax applicable in N.Y. Canadian residents will be charged applicable taxes. Offer not valid in Quebec. This offer is limited to one order per household. Not valid for current subscribers to Harlequin Special Edition books. All orders subject to credit approval. Credit or debit balances in a customer's account(s) may be offset by any other outstanding balance owed by or to the customer. Please allow 4 to 6 weeks for delivery. Offer available while quantities last.

Your Privacy—The Harlequin® Reader Service is committed to protecting your privacy. Our Privacy Policy is available online at www.ReaderService.com or upon request from the Harlequin Reader Service.

We make a portion of our mailing list available to reputable third parties that offer products we believe may interest you. If you prefer that we not exchange your name with third parties, or if you wish to clarify or modify your communication preferences, please visit us at www.ReaderService.com/consumerchoice or write to us at Harlequin Reader Service Preference Service, P.O. Box 9062, Buffalo, NY 14269. Include your complete name and address.

HSE13R

Jasmine "Jazzy" Cates looked at her time volunteering in Rust Creek Falls as an escape from the familiarity of Thunder Canyon. A fresh start. After a few months in town with no luck, she was about to give up. And then Brooks Smith, a sexy local veterinarian, makes a surprising proposal that just might solve all their problems…

***

Brooks knew he must be crazy.

Today he was going to marry a woman he was severely attracted to, yet he didn't intend to sleep with her! If that wasn't crazy, he didn't know what was.

He adjusted his tux, straightened his bolo tie, wishing all to heck that Jazzy hadn't almost knocked his boots off last night when he'd seen her in that red dress. And when he pushed her chair in and saw that hole in the back of it…and her skin peeking through, he'd practically swallowed his tongue.

There was a rap on the door. He was in the anteroom that led to the nursery area in the back of the church. He knew Jazzy was in a room across the vestibule that was used exactly for situations like this—brides and their bridesmaids preparing for a wedding.

Preparing for a wedding.

After the dinner last night, and the suspicious and wary glances of her family, he'd retreated inward. He knew that. He also knew it had bothered Jazzy. But how could he explain to her that she turned him on more than he'd ever wanted to be turned on? How could he explain to her that this marriage of convenience might not be so convenient, not when it came to them living together?

Still, he was determined to go through with this. Their course was set. He wasn't going to turn back now.

***

We hope you enjoyed this sneak peek from author Karen Rose Smith's new Harlequin® Special Edition book, MARRYING DR. MAVERICK, the next installment in MONTANA MAVERICKS: RUST CREEK COWBOYS, the brand-new six-book continuity launched in July 2013!